Author, poet and translator, **Deepa Agarwal**
writes for both children and adults and has fifty
published books to her credit. She has received
several awards for her work. Her picture book,
Ashok's New Friends, was awarded the National
Award for Children's Literature by the National
Council of Educational Research and Training
(NCERT), while the historical fiction *Caravan
to Tibet* featured on the International Board on
Books for Young People Honour List of 2008.

The Teenage Diary of

Nur Jahan

{ Mehr-un-nissa }

Deepa Agarwal

talking
CUB

TALKING CUB
Published by Speaking Tiger Publishing Pvt. Ltd
4381/4 Ansari Road, Daryaganj, New Delhi-110002, India

Published in Talking Cub by Speaking Tiger in paperback in 2019

ISBN: 978-93-88874-03-8
eISBN: 978-93-88874-02-1

10 9 8 7 6 5 4 3 2 1

Typeset in Goudy Old Style by Jojy Philip

The Teenage Diary of Nur Jahan

{ Mehr-un-nissa }

The Thirty-Fourth Year of the Reign of His Majesty Padshah Abul Fath Jalal-Ud-Din Muhammad Akbar

Kabul, 1 June 1590

AS I LOOK OUT OF MY WINDOW, I can catch a glimpse of the Kuh-e-sherdarwaza mountain blushing under the gaze of the setting sun. It is magical, watching that warm pink spread over the snowcapped peak. Below it, at one end, the Bala Hissar fortress looms on a hill, and the turreted mud wall that guards Kabul stretches out from its flanks like two arms enclosing the city.

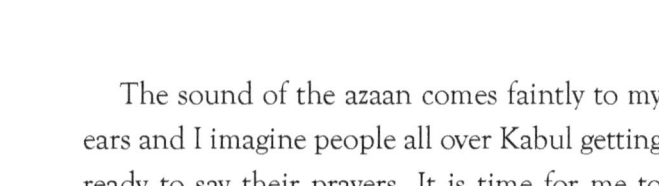

The sound of the azaan comes faintly to my ears and I imagine people all over Kabul getting ready to say their prayers. It is time for me to join my family, too.

Yesterday, by the grace of Allah, I, Mehr-un-nissa, daughter of Mirza Ghiyas Beg and Asmat Begum, completed thirteen years of existence on this earth. And more than one whole year in this Godforsaken place.

No, maybe I shouldn't say that. As much as I miss the bustle and activity, the pomp and splendour of Padshah Akbar's court, there are some things to recommend about this distant outpost of the Mughal empire. Distant, but very important. The Emperor's illustrious grandfather Babur came to love this city, which was the springboard of his destiny. Akbar himself was held hostage here by his uncle Mirza Kamran as a three-year-old. This was during the unfortunate time when his father Humayun was forced to go into exile to Persia after being ousted by Sher Shah Suri. Humayun returned in 1545 and conquered this city. And after rescuing his son, Humayun began his

triumphant return to Hindustan and ascended the Mughal throne again.

Thirteen years...I'm not sure how pleased I am to have reached this significant age. There are both advantages and disadvantages. For one thing, as my nurse Dilbagh proclaimed, I'm considered a woman now. That's an exciting thought, but then, there are responsibilities that accompany this state, and some are not so pleasant. Like being compelled to conceal my face under the veil in public, or when I appear before a man not considered maharam—one close enough to look upon the women of a family.

All the same, it is a milestone to be marked, so I've decided to begin a roznamcha—a diary— to record the important events of my day.

There is another reason—not just my love for putting pen to paper. The truth is, both my mind and my heart are so full of turmoil these days, that at times I feel ready to explode. But in whom can I confide and find relief? Ammi, loving as she is, would gently admonish me and advise me to be grateful for our continued good fortune. My father dotes on me, but I would hate

to burden him with my problems. My brothers are out of the question. As for my sisters—Saliha has got married and left. She is Sadiq Khan's wife now, preoccupied with her womanly duties. Khadija and Manija are practically babies. As for my maid Dilbagh, she shares so many other people's secrets when she's oiling and braiding my hair or preparing my bath—she's the last person any intelligent girl would choose as her confidante! And there isn't a single girl of my age here, whom I can call my friend.

Luckily, it occurred to me that I could unload my emotions on the pages of a diary. Writing your thoughts down relieves unhappiness, my last tutor, the one with that thrilling timbre in his voice, had said. All those heart-rending ghazals are the exquisite byproducts of sorrow. I was totally in agreement with him. How often have I crept away to inscribe a poem after my older brother Muhammad Sharif said something hurtful? Or when thoughts of the person whom I adore most on this earth and whose face I haven't beheld for over a year, torment me?

Frankly, I got the idea when Hasan Jamal, the same tutor, mentioned that highly placed people often maintain a daily diary or dictate one to a scribe to keep a record of their eventful lives. I had heard about the *Baburnama* earlier—the autobiography of the first Mughal emperor. In fact, the news is that Padshah Akbar's stepson and one of his Navratnas, Abdul Rahim Khan-i-khana, is translating that important work into Persian from the original Turki.

'It is almost complete,' our ataliq—tutor, informed us. 'They say it begins very simply, with the words, "*In the month of Ramadan of the year 899 and in the twelfth year of my age, I became ruler in the country of Farghana.*"'

'I hope we will get a chance to read it soon,' I said, trying to keep my voice even. Something about those words had sent a shiver up my spine.

Because...and this is a secret I'm sharing with you, diary, I have made up my mind that I, too, will attain a high position some day. Maybe it's time to get used to this activity.

When we arrived here, I must confess I felt

absolutely miserable, though I should have been proud that my father was granted this important position of the Diwan, or treasurer, of Kabul. But for me, to be away from the Mughal court is living death.

Not that I was so selfish as to make my unhappiness obvious. We were in Lahore then, and I had overheard my father telling my mother about it. When the imperial farman sealing the appointment arrived, I wasted no time in kissing my father's hand and said, 'Mubarak ho, Baba! May Allah always bless you with such honours and unending progress.'

Baba squeezed my hand between his large warm palms and put his lips to my bowed head. Ammi who was watching, smiled and my brothers, Muhammad Sharif and Abul Hasan followed suit. Muhammad flung a black look in my direction because I had been so quick thinking and taken the lead. I pretended I hadn't noticed. My sisters Saliha, Khadija and Manija lined up behind them. Little Shahpur, my youngest brother too.

I had been tempted to recite a poem I had

just composed but decided to save it for another occasion.

'It is a great honour, dear children,' my sweet mother beamed. 'Kabul is one of the most important cities in the empire. It is a beautiful place, full of gardens and surrounded by mountains. We will be away from the killing heat of Lahore and Agra.'

'Why did the Padshah decide to send you there, Baba?' Muhammad asked ungraciously. 'So far from the court. All the important things happen here.'

'Because he has great regard for me,' my father replied patiently. 'Zille Illahi trusts me. "We find none other than you suitable for the post, Mirza Ghiyas Beg," he said. "Kabul is dear to us Mughals, you well know. Our respected grandfather Babur began his imperial career from Kabul. We wish to see the revenues of our ancestral place well administered."'

'It feels more like exile,' Muhammad continued to grumble.

If my mother hadn't called out to a maid to bring some sweets to celebrate the occasion, he

would have got into an argument. Always surly, my oldest brother. Not Abul though. Though he is almost twenty, he is full of mischief. He seems to have an endless stock of jokes stored in his head.

Why can't Muhammad be more like that, I sometimes think. But I have begun to understand that though this earth is full of delights such as the pistachio barfis Ammi passed around, the splendour of the court, and handsome young princes like Shehzada Salim, there are bitter people to remind us that we are living on earth, not paradise.

'Asmat, you will have to begin packing soon,' my father's eyes were distant and thoughtful, as he took a sip of his favourite khus sherbat.

At that time, I couldn't help thinking of the lovely silk peshwaz Ammi had got me just the day before—sky blue, to match my eyes. The bodice was embroidered with sequins that would twinkle through the muslin robe on top. There is a matching shalwar with a border of intricate embroidery. Would there be any occasions to flaunt it in the wilds of Kabul?

'You are suddenly gaining height, Mehru,' Ammi had smiled, when she ordered it. 'Outgrowing all your clothes.'

'Give them to Manija,' I said. 'They are practically new.'

'Why should I wear your cast-off clothes?' Manija pouted.

Ammi had laughed and chucked my sister under her chin. 'Your sister's joking, Manija. By God's grace, your father does not lack the resources to keep all his children in new clothes.'

It's hard to imagine that a year has passed by since then. But I hear someone at the door. I should hide this away. My thoughts, my words may be innocent enough but they are my secrets. I can't bear to think what might happen if my diary fell into the wrong hands.

A week later

So dear roznamcha, once we fell into a routine, I started getting used to this place. I kept consoling myself that sooner or later the Padshah would call Baba back to court. He values his services too much. The only problem was how soon?

If too many years passed, would the Padshah Begum Ruqayya forget me? I would never find a chance to cross paths with Prince Salim then, whom I have admired for a long time.

The first time I set eyes on him, I was just a little girl. Ammi had taken me to the palace at Agra with her—I had been asking so many questions about it. The Emperor was holding court and we had thronged to the latticed marble screens to watch. The Padshah sat on his golden jewel-studded throne, with a pigeon nestling against his chest. I blinked at the sight of the dazzling jewels on his turban and the numerous necklaces looped around his neck. He looked so kind, but there was a muscular strength to his body that impressed me even then. At the distance of say a few yards, on his right sat a young man. His dress was even more splendid, if possible.

'Can you see the shehzada?' One of the jostling women exclaimed.

'As handsome as ever,' the other sighed. 'Look at his magnificent qaba, covered all over with gold embroidery.'

'And those enormous ruby buttons!'

I craned my neck to get a closer look. Yes, with his elaborately ornamented turban and a jewel-studded dagger tucked into his cummerbund, Salim looked every inch a prince.

Bursting with excitement, when I got home, I bragged to my brothers. 'I saw the Padshah... and the shehzada today. He was covered with gold from head to toe.'

'Covered with gold!' Muhammad and Abul looked at each other and burst out laughing. 'Covered with gold, ha, ha!' Abul repeated. It became a joke with them. After that, whenever I went to the palace, they would teasingly ask, 'Did you see the shehzada? Was he covered with gold?'

Fed up, one day I said defiantly, 'Yes, I see him every day! I am going to marry him and he will punish you for tormenting me!'

They laughed even harder and I burst into tears. Ammi scolded them to stop it at once. But the seed of my fascination had been planted. My eyes always searched for Salim at the monthly Meena Bazaar. Once Ammi and I actually came face to face with him. But we simply performed a low kornish and backed away. He didn't even get a proper look at us, I think.

Thinking of this, I got a brilliant idea. Perhaps if I kept writing to the Padshah Begum, she might mention me to the shehzada. 'Do you remember that lovely girl with brilliant blue eyes, Sheikhu Baba?' she might say. That's how his father addresses him—Sheikhu Baba. Apparently, none of the Emperor's children had survived till he visited saint Sheikh Salimuddin Chishti at Fatehpur Sikri and asked for his blessings. When the prince was born, he was named 'Salim' after the saint. But Akbar lovingly calls him Sheikhu Baba. 'She has written to me from Kabul,' I can imagine the Empress telling him. 'She has enclosed a charming ghazal too, quite mature for a thirteen-year-old girl.'

The thought cheered me up so much that I wasted no time in beginning the letter, even though it was almost time for our tutor to arrive. Later, I managed to snatch time to complete it. Then it struck me that I needed

to ask my father if it was appropriate for me to write to the Empress.

But her majesty had said, hadn't she, 'I will miss you, Mehr-un-nissa. Keep sending me news from Kabul'?

Argh...how can I write down my thoughts while Dilbagh Bi is breaking down the door? They think there's something sinful about a girl wanting to spend time by herself. I'm lucky to have the excuse that solitude is essential to compose poetry. And Baba insists that it's essential for a girl from an aristocratic family to be well versed in the creative arts, to be able to pen verses, paint pictures, study music apart from being proficient in other branches of learning. Don't the Mughal empresses and princesses compose poetry all the time?

And I definitely want to shine in all the arts. My knowledge of literature in all the important languages—Turkish, Farsee and Arabic—has impressed our new tutor I can see.

Hai Allah! The old woman has begun to screech out my name at the top of her voice. Time to run!

A fortnight later

It is hard to say whom I love more—my mother or my father. Truly, I have been blessed to have such affectionate parents. Ammi's life is completely devoted to the well-being of our family. Her whole day passes in thinking about our meals, our lessons, our clothes, our entertainment. However, while we were in Agra or Lahore, she could hold her own at court as well as any aristocratic lady.

Baba, though he is bowed down by the weight of his important but difficult assignment, always finds time for us, even if it is to enquire about our day at the evening meal. Between mouthfuls of naan dipped in lamb salan or chewing a marrow bone, he will ask, 'What new topic did your tutor take up today?'

I'm always the first to speak up. I don't care that it makes Muhammad bhai unhappy. I know, even if I didn't, he would still be dissatisfied. So, whether it's astronomy or the metre used in a masnavi verse, I do not hesitate to discuss it with Baba. The depth of his knowledge never

fails to amaze me. But then, he belongs to a family of famous poets.

When I was younger, I didn't care to find out too much about our family roots. It was enough to know that we had come from Persia. Fled rather, to escape my father's enemies. And that I had been born on the way at Kandahar. It didn't seem important to dig further.

But during our long journey from Lahore to Kabul, I couldn't help noticing that on and off, deep lines would etch themselves on Baba's face. I thought he was filled with anxiety about his new assignment, even though it was unlike him. The way his gaze lingered on certain spots, the way he glanced around him and sighed, it appeared as if he was dredging up memories—not very happy ones. My heart begins to sink if I see even the faintest of shadows on my beloved father's face. So, I decided to question him in the evening, after we girls had dismounted from our camel howdah.

That is how we travelled to Kabul, on the backs of camels, with the men keeping pace on their horses. I waited till the tents had been unfolded and set up, the carpets spread out on the bare earth and Baba was reclining comfortably against a bolster, puffing at his hookah. I crept into his tent and curled up at his feet. He stroked my head gently. 'Forgive me, Baba, for my impertinence,' I had begun hesitantly, 'but you seem very preoccupied. Has the Emperor handed you a very complicated task to perform?'

I could hear the crackle of kitchen fires being lit nearby and the head cook shouting to his helpers. Somewhere one of our guards was belting out a rollicking folksong.

'It is not that, my child,' my father had smiled wanly. 'You know I consider myself equal to almost any task our gracious Padshah might entrust me with.' Then he had sighed deeply. 'Why hide it from you? I-I am plagued with old memories that haunt me like ghosts.'

'Baba...' I had asked hesitantly, 'is this the same route you took when you were travelling to Hindustan?'

'Almost...' he smiled again. 'One day, when

you are older, I will tell you the story of our journey to Hindustan.'

I am twelve, Baba, I had wanted to cry out. Old enough. By this age many girls get married. But the dark cloud that hung over his brow discouraged me. Maybe I should wait. Hadn't Baba said, over and over again, patience is a great virtue? And maybe, I could find an opportunity to ask Ammi.

Preferably when none of my siblings were around, I decided, because just that moment Abul had slipped into the tent. I am sure he was curious about my conversation with Baba.

'This place abounds in deer, Baba,' he said eagerly. 'Can we take time off for a short hunting foray tomorrow? Our cook is such an expert in preparing game. Maybe we can bag some wild fowl as well.'

'All right,' Baba said. 'Since our progress has been good and the weather is pleasant.'

'Can I try a few shots too, Baba?' I spoke up immediately.

'Of course, my dear girl,' Baba's eyes gleamed with amusement. I was glad that Abul's request

had pulled him out of his gloom. And also pleased to find an opportunity to improve my marksmanship. Many of the court ladies were skilled not only in archery but also accomplished at handling guns. In fact, Prince Salim's Rajput wife Jagat Gosaini is famous for her accuracy.

I didn't want to be any less than her.

A few days later

It had taken me some time to feel as comfortable in this house as we were in my father's mansions in Agra and Fatehpur Sikri. But Kabul's natural beauty, the breathtaking sight of the snowcapped mountains with the Kabul river's crystal-clear waters flowing through the city, won my heart. I longed to go for a picnic to one of the enchanting gardens I had heard so much about, some built by Mughal princesses. But my mother couldn't relax till all our furniture and other belongings had been unpacked and the kitchen properly equipped. She bustled around seeing that the expensive carpets were unrolled and the cold stone floors acquired the warmth of their colours. The paintings had to be hung on the walls and the porcelain and silver knick-knacks arranged for effect. She even draped a couple of the embroidered phulkari sheets we had brought from Lahore. Visitors needed to be aware that they were not entering an ordinary man's home.

It was the home of Mirza Ghiyas Beg, a Persian noble and the treasurer of Kabul, appointed by none less than the most powerful man in the world as we know it—the Mughal Emperor Akbar Shah.

This place abounds in a variety of delicious fruits like the most honeyed melons and grapes, luscious figs, apricots, peaches and pears. I have heard about peaches as large as an owl's head, and other fantastic fruit. When a basket of dark red pomegranates arrived today, Dilbagh smiled and said, 'Huzoor, pomegranates from Kandahar. How fresh and juicy they are!'

Ammi smiled. 'Tell the kitchen maid to shell them immediately.'

'Kandahar!' I cried. 'Isn't that the place of my birth?'

Ammi became pensive. 'Yes, jaan,' she said. 'It is.'

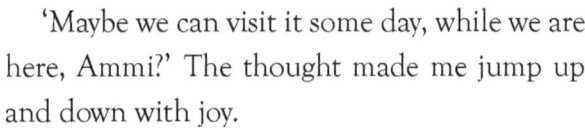

'Maybe we can visit it some day, while we are here, Ammi?' The thought made me jump up and down with joy.

'My dear, Kandahar is occupied by the Persian Shah,' Ammi said quietly. 'It is hostile territory for us.'

'Ohh...' It was disappointing to hear that.

Later in the afternoon, as we lounged in the zenana baithak, savouring the sweetness of pomegranate seeds, I couldn't help thinking of my birthplace again. A question flashed into my mind. 'Why did we leave Persia, Ammi?'

The two of us were alone by chance. The boys had gone out riding and my little sisters were busy with their dolls.

Ammi hesitated for a moment. Then she sighed heavily and said, 'Perhaps it is time to share this story with you, painful as it is. You are almost a woman. You need to know how one's fortunes can change, in a split second. That this prosperity we take for granted is not necessarily permanent.'

I turned cold. For a moment I felt sorry I had asked. But my insatiable curiosity will never

give me peace. And the remarks the ladies at the court let drop sometimes, not always kind, had sharpened it. I had heard remarks such as, 'The Persian adventurer has really advanced by leaps and bounds.'

Sometimes when Baba was distributing food to the poor, he would say, 'Mehr, Allah has blessed us with so much, we must remember to share his gifts with those less fortunate.'

The undercurrent in his voice made me uneasy. Doing charity was a religious duty, but there was an intensity in Baba and Ammi when they performed these acts that made it different from the routine manner in which most of the courtiers gave alms.

'Your grandfather, Muhammad Sharif, was in favour with Shah Tahmasp Safavi of Persia,' my mother began in an expressionless tone. 'He was the wazir of Isfahan when he passed away, just a year before you were born. When the Shah too died, his successor Shah Ismad II turned against us. We had to flee Tehran for our lives at dead of night. Your father decided to seek his fortune in India and we joined a caravan. But...' to my

dismay, she brushed at her eye, 'we were waylaid by robbers and lost everything. Our gold and silver, jewels, even our horses.'

My blood seemed to freeze in my veins. This was far worse than I could have imagined. I almost reached out to place a hand on my mother's mouth and cry out, 'Stop, Ammi!' but I dug my teeth into my lower lip. However horrifying, this was a story I needed to know.

'We managed to get hold of two mules, which we rode in turns. Your brothers and sister were very young, and I was in the last stage of my pregnancy. We almost begged our way to Kandahar.' Ammi tried to smile through her tears. My heart was thudding painfully.

'Some nomads gave us shelter. And when my labour pains began, an old midwife helped to deliver you.' Ammi's eyes spilled over when she said, 'I thought you were the most beautiful baby ever born.'

I choked on my own tears and nestled closer to my mother, inhaling the scent of her favourite attar. The pomegranate seeds glowed in the silver bowl like rubies. An unrelated

thought went through my mind: Prince Salim loved rubies, I had heard.

Ammi squeezed me tight. 'Mehru, jaan, don't hate us for what I'm going to tell you next.'

'Can I ever hate you?' I was shrill in my protest. 'May Allah strike me dead if I ever do!'

'Listen!' my mother hissed fiercely.

I was terrified. I had never heard my gentle mother speak in such a tone. I clutched a cushion for support. She went on, without looking at me. 'The most beautiful baby...but we had little food to eat, so...I had no milk to feed you. You began to waste away before our eyes...Our fortunes had improved somewhat by then as we had joined the caravan of the gracious Malik Masud. But still, we hardly had any money for food. Rather than watch you starve slowly, we decided to abandon you, hoping that someone better off might find you and take care of you.'

Ammi's voice broke at this point. I should have screamed or burst into a paroxysm of weeping. But it suddenly felt as if someone had placed a large rock on my heart, crushing all emotion.

'Go on, Ammi,' I said calmly. 'What happened next?'

Ammi's eyes opened wide. She stared at me as though I was a stranger. Then she drew a deep breath. 'Your father left you under a tree, praying that someone would find you soon... and...his prayers were answered. Malik Masud himself found you. He-he charged us to take care of you and gave your father money for your upkeep. Allah restored you to us, my child! You were lucky for us, extremely lucky...'

This story walloped me with its weight. I tried to embrace Ammi, hold her close as she wept, but I was in a daze, rather in a kind of trance. Only when my little sisters ran into the room, along with our brother Shahpur, clamouring for some pomegranate, did my trance break.

Two days later

I have not been able to write anything for two days. My head is stuffed with some peculiar matter, something so dense that nothing else can enter.

It is not that I have begun to hate my parents

as my mother had feared. I can see her sad eyes fixed on me, trying to decipher my expression. I should have reassured her. But it was as if words, speech, laughter and poetry—everything that came to me so easily—had deserted me.

That evening at dinner, Baba asked, 'What's the matter, Mehru? You're very quiet today.'

'Nothing, Baba,' I stretched my lips into the semblance of a smile. 'I have a slight headache.'

'Maybe a poem is hatching inside her,' Abul grinned, his mouth stuffed with biryani. 'She's like a broody hen.'

I glared at him, trying to fight my nausea. The sight of all that food turned my stomach suddenly, thinking of my mother starving after my birth. Me, wasting away for lack of milk. But I was lucky, Ammi said.

Yes, I was definitely lucky and would get even luckier. Pulling myself together, I turned my frown into a smile and said:

'Does rain simply fall from the skies?
think of the cloud that carried it in its womb,
roaming the firmament laden with its weight,

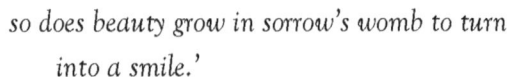

so does beauty grow in sorrow's womb to turn into a smile.'

'Irshad! Mashallah, my dear, you are truly a poet's granddaughter!' my father exclaimed. 'This poem deserves a gift. Ask what you will.'

I hesitated. The sight of the smile on Ammi's tired face was reward enough. 'Ask,' my father repeated, 'what would you like, jaan? A necklace of pearls or the jade bracelet the jeweller brought the other day. Or would you prefer a silken soft pashmina shawl?'

'The shawl, Baba,' I said quickly, 'a plain one, so I can embroider it myself, with a pattern I am designing right now.'

'You need to burn chillies to ward off the evil eye,' old Dilbagh croaked. 'This girl has too many talents. May she live to grow old.'

'She will, bi.' Baba's face grew pensive. 'She has already proved her talent for survival.'

I salaamed my father in gratitude, then concentrated on washing my hands. As Dilbagh poured warm rose-scented water from a silver jug over my fingers while another maid held a

silver basin beneath them, I thought, I don't need that many talents to achieve my goal in life. My blue eyes are enough. But it makes life more interesting if you can sing and paint, embroider and compose poetry.

A week later

The more I think about it, Ammi's revelation evokes even greater tenderness in me towards my parents. To think that my successful, courtly father had experienced dire poverty and such despair! It made him far more human and vulnerable. Was it really the good fortune my birth brought that had catapulted him up the ladder in Padshah Akbar's court? It was a slippery ladder, with so many people constantly trying to drag you down. It was an extremely taxing game of wits and swift maneuvering.

'I began with a mansab of three hundred soldiers,' he would say. 'By God's grace, I have reached this position. God's grace, Malik Masud's help and Zille Illahi's kindness.'

It helped that the Empress had received us kindly too and we had been warmly welcomed by Salima Sultana Begum, the other senior wife. While Ruqayya Begum is the Emperor's cousin and they have practically grown up together, Salima Sultana is also related to him. She was originally married to Bairam Khan, the Emperor's guardian, who was murdered. Ruqayya has no children but she has always been the favourite wife. Thanks to their goodwill, we became frequent visitors to the zenana while Baba won the Emperor's favour with his witty conversation and intelligent advice.

Now that the story had been filled out further, I became convinced that the destiny of our family was linked to that of the Mughal dynasty.

Yes, Salim is meant for me! There, I've said it. I am convinced I was born to wield power like the Padshah Begum.

Hai Allah, what a fool I am! What have I written! I had better scratch these words out. No one should read them. But will it bring bad luck to erase them? I will take the risk!

But now Ammi is calling. No lessons today! We are to visit Bagh-e-Babur, the garden created

by Salim's illustrious great grandfather and pay our respects at his tomb. We have been there a few times already, but it is a place that can never lose its fascination for me. I love visiting the other enchanting gardens created by Mughal princesses, too. What a wonderful experience it must be to design a garden! And to design a building, that must be even more fulfilling.

The next day

Whenever we leave the confines of our courtyard and enter the bustling streets of Kabul, I can't help thinking how different it is to Lahore or Agra—in the people, language, weather and surroundings. The towering Hindukush mountains provide such an impressive backdrop to the city and the Kabul river adds a gentle, peaceful note. Donkeys carrying melons and pomegranates, grandly dressed men riding horses, women with baskets of vegetables for sale or water pots—that is not so different.

Peeping from between the curtains of my palanquin, I always strain my ears to catch the conversation of the tall, bearded men in their peaked turbans or astrakhan caps. I can decipher the occasional Persian or Turki familiar to us but there are many tribes living in this region, thus many different dialects. They say you can hear at least twelve languages in Kabul—Arabic, Persian, Turki, Hindi, Pashto and several others. Apart from the Afghans, there are a large number of Tajiks, Hazaras and Pashtuns. Some, like the Hazaras, are Shia like us, I have heard, but most are Sunnis.

It was not as humid as Lahore or Agra would be in August. The sun was bright but it was fairly windy. If we were in Agra, we might have been watching the dark clouds rolling over the sky while we swung to and fro under the trees. The Hindus celebrate this season with all kinds of festivities. We would be singing the songs of Sawan and decorating our palms with henna. The sky would be colourful with kites. Even Padshah Akbar likes to fly kites. They don't have the monsoon rains here, but it snows in winter. That was an exciting new experience—to wake up to a world that had donned a mantle of white overnight.

As usual, we had carried a picnic lunch—melt-in-your-mouth kababs, naan, a delectable lamb biryani and many other dainties. For some reason, I could not help recalling the hundred dishes prepared in the Padshah's kitchen every day. He may be a frugal eater, but the kitchen runs all night in case the ladies of the harem fancy some refreshment.

Babur's tomb with its upright latticed panels inspires a kind of awe. He was not originally buried here; I've been told his remains were brought from Agra so he could rest in a place he had learned to love. The same uncanny feeling that had gripped me the first time we visited, came over me, as we stood with our hands upraised in prayer. The opening words of Babur's biography sketched themselves in my mind. Babur had mounted the throne at the age of twelve. Our Padshah too was barely thirteen when anointed as the emperor of Hindustan.

An aura of energy seemed to waft from the tomb, of immense power. Babur had established a new empire and Akbar had expanded it to

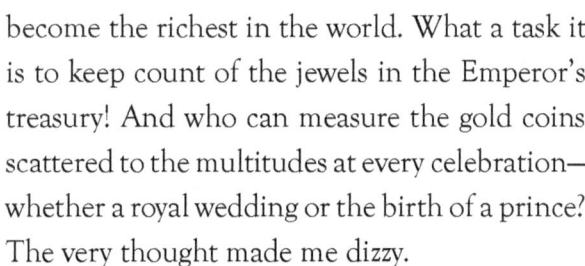

become the richest in the world. What a task it is to keep count of the jewels in the Emperor's treasury! And who can measure the gold coins scattered to the multitudes at every celebration— whether a royal wedding or the birth of a prince? The very thought made me dizzy.

After we had prayed there, I looked around at the symmetrical rows of trees and flowering shrubs that surrounded it. This was one of Emperor Babur's favourite spots, apparently, and he had a guest house here. I could understand why. With the spectacular backdrop of the mountains and the muted murmur of the water channel that neatly divided the garden, there was something tranquil about it.

As the servants erected the tent inside which we were to sit, Khadija, Manija and Shahpur began to frolic on the grass like little fawns. Their shalwars flapped around their legs as they tried to catch butterflies and I could not help smiling at the sight.

Muhammad had excused himself today, but Abul accompanied us. 'How is it that you're so quiet today, Mehru?' he asked, his eyes twinkling.

'Ammi, I'm surprised that she's sitting here with us, instead of racing her sisters?'

'Abul,' my mother frowned, 'Mehr-un-nissa is not a child any longer. She has to maintain decorum.'

I sighed. The prospect of strolling around the gardens muffled in a cumbersome veil quite ruined the pleasure of being here on this breezy day. I would have liked to clamber up the hillock in front of us to enjoy a better view of the gardens, but Ammi would not have found such actions appropriate.

That's the price girls have to pay for growing up.

All the same, it was a delight to inhale the scent of the roses blooming so profusely and the raw tang of apples ripening on the trees. And as I said, the water flowing down the channels had a lovely, soothing sound.

I began to play a game by myself: to redesign the garden to my taste. I shifted the flower beds and rearranged the trees and shrubs. Was that very presumptuous on my part? Perhaps...but princess or commoner, we are all entitled to dream...

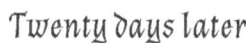

Twenty days later

Our routine has been pretty well fixed for the past year. From 10 a.m. to 1 p.m. we study the languages, mathematics and the scriptures. This ataliq says it's important to study history as well. Every time I visit Emperor Babur's tomb, my fascination for the story of his conquest of Hindustan is rekindled. Valour, confidence and determination: isn't that what human beings need to succeed? Perseverance too. He set a goal for himself and he achieved it.

My lessons are behind purdah, since the tutor is a man. This doesn't stop me from asking questions. Don't the court ladies in the zenana speak out their minds from behind the marble jalis in court, when they have an opinion to contribute?

At the court, every day was different. There were grand celebrations at festivals and weddings and the births of babies in the royal household and among the nobility. There was news of fresh military campaigns and conquests as the Emperor had set out to extend his domains and was busy subduing

rulers of all the regions around him. Wasn't the magnificent Buland Darwaza at Fatehpur Sikri built to commemorate his victory over Gujarat? Kabul itself was wrenched from his brother Mirza Muhammad Hakim after which his sister Bakht-un-nissa Begum was made governor.

Most fascinating of all was to observe the visitors from distant parts of the world presenting themselves to the Emperor at his Diwan-i-khas. We would goggle through the lattices of the women's enclosure at their outlandish costumes and puzzle at the pink faces of the Portuguese priests who had been trying to win the Emperor over to their religion for a long time.

I must mention here, that the way the Emperor conducts himself is always mesmerizing. Whether he is receiving dignitaries or listening to the pleas of the common people at his jharokha darshan, when he stands at his balcony to let the public catch a glimpse of the ruler of their destinies. He is regal and dignified and has such a pleasant expression, even the mole on his left upper lip makes him appear

distinguished. He looks so much like the loving grandfather he is, that it's hard to imagine that he can be cruel and unforgiving to his enemies and that he even threw his foster brother Adham Khan off the roof to his death. The man had exceeded the bounds of insolence, my tutor said. If an emperor does not demonstrate his preeminence, how will he control his domain?

In Kabul, the monotony gets to me at times. This morning when I asked Baba if I could accompany him and my brothers on their morning ride, he exchanged glances with my mother then said, 'It is better that you don male attire and mask your face.'

'What does she need to go riding for?' Muhammad Sharif frowned.

'It's all right, son,' my father said gently. 'Your sister feels the need for exercise too, the way you do. It's good for her to hone her horse-riding skills.'

'You spoil her,' my brother protested.

'Enough!' Baba said sternly. 'I make the rules in this house. Don't forget that.'

This exchange spoiled my mood a bit but a

good gallop cured that. I managed to get the feel of the wind on my face!

Two days later

Delicious aromas are wafting from the kitchen. Cardamom, cinnamon, saffron, rose water, musk...

As I rose from my morning prayers, I asked Dilbagh, 'Is there a festival that I've forgotten?'

She cackled. 'Do you only get fancy fare at festivals, child? We are expecting a special guest today. A very special one indeed...your benefactor.'

'Is-is it Malik Masud sahib?' I cried.

'No less.' Dilbagh looked at me shrewdly. It was almost as if she was trying to tell me something. But I wanted to talk to Ammi right then.

It was three years since I had last met Malik Masud. He had visited our house in Agra and Ammi and Baba had welcomed him like royalty. The most sumptuous dishes our kitchen could produce, the best Chinese porcelain and silverware had been laid out. Baba had

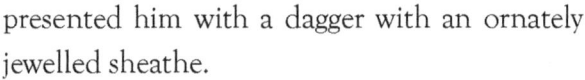

presented him with a dagger with an ornately jewelled sheathe.

'All the jewels in Hindustan cannot repay our debt to you,' he had said.

'But where is my little jewel?' Malik Masud sahib had asked.

I was hiding behind a screen and had run out as if on cue. I knew the elderly merchant had a special fondness for me, but it is only now, after Ammi told me the story that I can understand why.

That day, I had remained dry eyed. But today, I needed to find a secluded spot to let my tears flow and relieve my overfull heart. And...I too wanted to give this special person a gift. But what could I offer?

'Ammi, Ma!' I almost bumped into Gulnar, my mother's personal maid as she came out of the store room, laden with huge silver salvers.

'Ya Allah! What is it, my child?' Ammi asked, tucking her huge bunch of keys into her waist.

'Is-is Malik Masud Miyan expected today?' I burst out.

Ammi smiled at my impetuosity, then

a shadow darkened her brow. There was a pleading look in her eyes. 'Ammi,' I said gently, 'I-I wanted to present a small gift to my saviour...' my voice faltered. It was not my intention to load my mother with guilt.

She nodded, then sighed deeply. 'It is a noble thought.'

'But what can I give?' Suddenly, I felt inadequate. Anything I offered, no matter how valuable, would not be enough to repay my debt.

Then my mother's face brightened. 'I know,' she said. 'That pashmina shawl you just finished embroidering. It will make the perfect gift.'

My heart leapt. 'Ammi!' I cried as I hugged her. 'You manage to find solutions for almost every problem.'

My mother smiled and patted my cheek. The shawl was to be a gift for Baba, but I can make another for him. After all, the person who saved me for my parents does not visit us every day.

'Ammi...maybe I can outline some of the flowers in golden thread to make it more special?'

'Be quick then, jaan!'

A fortnight later

So much has been happening lately that I have barely been able to squeeze out a private moment to write my diary. Today...I am being forced to rest so I have a rare opportunity to sort out my tangled thoughts and mull over the many events of the last fortnight.

First of course is Malik Masud's visit.

Since he is like family, I was not required to veil myself, which was both a relief and not. Not, because I was so overwhelmed when I saw him and it was hard to hide it. He has aged a lot. His beard is almost white now and he seems to drag his steps.

'Who is this young lady?' he asked, when I bent low to offer my salaam. He looked genuinely surprised. 'Mirza Ghiyas Beg, you will soon have to find a bridegroom for this priceless jewel.'

Baba tried to smile. Suddenly I felt shy. My face went hot and I knew everyone must have noticed that I was blushing. That embarrassed me even more. Maybe it would have been better if I had been veiled.

'Her older sister has been settled,' said my father. 'By Allah's grace we found a worthy young man for Saliha. And Muhammad too will be wed. I hope you will be here to witness the nikah next month, Mirza Masud.'

'Mubarak ho! How can I miss such an auspicious occasion?' Our benefactor beamed from ear to ear. 'Come, let me bless you, son.'

My brother Muhammad looks quite handsome when he smiles. I wish he would smile more.

It was only after dinner that I was able to overcome my inhibitions to present my gift. That too after Ammi said, 'Masud sahib, your jewel has a small gift for you. Something she has made herself.'

With downcast eyes, I placed the shawl in his hands. There was much I wanted to say, but my throat had clamped itself shut. The look that travelled between Malik Masud and me lasted only a split second, but it said all. 'May your kismet carry you to a place higher than we can imagine, my child,' he murmured, placing a hand on my head.

It felt as if a shower of stars had fallen all around me.

Ten days later

When we first came here, I thought I would die of boredom. And as I mentioned earlier, sometimes I still feel like that. But all of a sudden, events seem to be multiplying—I can barely stop to draw breath before something new turns up. First Saliha's wedding and now Muhammad's. Visitors from court arrive bringing news of all kinds of developments and of course, Salim's recent marriage alliances.

Well, he is a prince. He will take many wives. If, as a baby I could survive a cobra, what threat could his other wives pose to my dreams?

It was Dilbagh who came out with the story. I wonder why my mother left out this part that day. I think it frightened her too much. Maybe it was better. There is only so much that a person can assimilate at a time.

It was a couple of days after Malik Masud visited. We were in a tizzy, putting the finishing touches on our gifts for Muhammad's bride.

I had undertaken to embroider a veil, using a design I had sketched out on an idle evening. My favourite sprigs of bela surrounded with a tracery of winding stems and delicate leaves, in gold and silver thread, interspersed with seed pearls. The material was flame red, a gauzy muslin Ammi had bought from a merchant who hawked fabrics from places as distant as Bengal. Our other maid Gulnar, who has a neat hand, was helping me.

Dilbagh paused to admire our work. 'Mashallah, you have been blessed with many talents,' she said. 'Sometimes I wonder if you are human or some supernatural being in disguise!'

I burst out laughing. 'Dilbagh bi, please don't say such things. Baba will be very annoyed.'

Dilbagh rolled her eyes, touched her ears, then continued in a whisper. 'Could a human baby survive the deadly coils of a cobra?'

Gulnar shrieked. She had pierced her finger with a needle. 'What are you talking about?' I said angrily. 'Have you lost your mind?'

'Ask Miyan Malik Masud then. He was the one who witnessed the sight. That is the

condition in which he found you. The cobra slithered away after he arrived.'

'I will,' I snapped, when I had recovered from the shock. 'And he's sure to tell me it's a figment of your mind. Cobra indeed! You can go now!'

Dilbagh left, shaking her head. 'She has an overactive imagination,' I told the pale-faced Gulnar.

'Yes...she is always full of tales of jinns and paris,' Gulnar tried to smile. 'Always suggesting visits to pirs to get charms and tabizes.' But it was obvious that she was uneasy.

I tried to make up for the interruption by pulling the needle through the fabric at top speed. The story, true or not, had chilled me. Should I ask my mother? I decided not to. It would only open up the old wound again.

The next day

How I wish Dilbagh had not come up with that cobra story. I had deliberately dismissed it as a fanciful tale but it brought on a terrible nightmare last night. I dreamt that an enormous

cobra had me in its coils. No matter how hard I struggled, I couldn't break free. I was choking, barely able to scream for help, when a gleaming figure appeared out of the mist that surrounded me. A heavenly angel! It slashed at the snake with a fiery sword and set me free. At that moment I came awake, in the grip of an uncontrollable shivering fit. My heart was thumping madly and I was soaked in sweat. Worst of all, I could still feel the imprint of those fearsome scales on my skin...

The dream possessed me like a curse the whole morning. I tried to recall what the zenana women who interpreted dreams used to say. Vaguely I remembered that they believed that a dream of snakes meant enemies were trying to harm you. But whose enmity had I provoked?

I prayed with great fervour that day.

A month later—October

The weather is beginning to change. The snow caps on the mountains seem to be travelling downhill rapidly. Ammi has started to harangue the servants to air out the quilts and warm clothes—the quilted jackets and fur-lined poshteen coats and woollen hats. Winter is rainy here. But I love the cold weather. To ride out with a bracing wind in your face, or let the hearty shorba of goat's trotters that Aslam, our head cook, prepares spread its warmth through your bones. And inside the house, the bukharis and coal braziers keep us snug and warm.

When Saliha left us, I didn't realize I would miss my quiet sister so much. Sometimes I envy her, in the midst of a busy social life, decked out in her trousseau outfits—shimmering robes of muslin and silk, her diamonds and rubies bringing a sparkle to her shy gaze. What will my new sister-in-law be like? Will she be a friend to me?

We receive regular news of the court. The Empress, however, has not replied to any of my letters. She is busy as ever, I'm sure. But it hurts that I matter so little to her.

I need to distract myself. There are my lessons, my poetry, painting and embroidery of course. But so often I wish I was a boy like Muhammad or Abul. That I could also take

part in the affairs of state, command troops and govern provinces. If I got a chance, I'm sure I'd be as good as anyone else.

Sometimes, Baba works late into the night. Managing the financial affairs of this large province is not an easy task. He has to be very careful too, Abul had told me once. The Emperor has spies who watch all his officials to be sure they are performing their duties conscientiously and there is no discrepancy in the accounts.

The treasury lies just next door to our house. Often, he is there till dusk has fallen, counting the sacks of mohurs and rupees brought in by the revenue collectors. Each and every coin has to be accounted for till the last copper dam and damdi. Then the treasury has to be locked up securely.

Last night I was particularly restless, so I decided to roam the house to calm myself. Then I saw the lamp burning in my father's study.

'Baba, you're still awake?' I whispered. 'You'll get very tired.'

'So are you, my dear,' he smiled. 'I need

to finish checking all these accounts. I have summoned the concerned officials tomorrow.'

I glanced down at the rows of figures. 'May I help, Baba? Then your work will be completed and we can both go to bed.' When he looked doubtful, I continued. 'It-it will be good practice for me too, to improve my skill with numbers.'

'A skill with numbers is equally important for women. I have seen how well the Mughal princesses manage their vast properties,' Baba nodded slowly. 'You are indeed my greatest blessing, Mehru. Here, just check these figures.'

I sat next to him and tried to decipher the rows of numbers. It took me a little while to get the hang of it and then I noticed it—something that didn't tally between the ledgers and the vouchers submitted. 'Baba...there seems to be a discrepancy here...' I said hesitantly, handing him the large bahi register awkwardly.

Baba pursed his lips. 'I did feel something was not right in these numbers,' he said slowly. 'God bless you, my child! It's possible that fellow is dipping his fist into the funds. I will take him to task tomorrow.'

'Baba, can I help you every day?' I asked excitedly.

'When there is extra work,' he replied with a smile. 'I cannot deprive you of your night's rest, child.'

That was not the last time I helped Baba in checking his accounts. It was fascinating to discover the process of collecting taxes and then deciding where to use the funds: for improving the lives of the citizens, constructing roads and serais, or digging wells and maintaining law and order. Sometimes I felt that too much money was spent on the troops.

'You can never spend too much money for your defence,' my father said gravely when I shared my opinion. 'Look at the years our great Emperor has spent in the saddle building this immense empire. Risking his life, subduing his enemies and thus extending his territories. He has shifted his capital to Lahore to keep the Uzbeks and Persians in check. If our neighbours get the impression that our defences are not strong, they will overrun Hindustan at the first opportunity.' He must have noticed the frown

on my face because he went on, 'It's true we are Persians, my dear, but now that I am in service of Padshah Akbar of Hindustan, I will look out for his interests. Your birthplace Kandahar is under Safavid rule. The Emperor is keen to bring it under his control. The further our boundaries extend, the safer for the common public.'

This was my first glimpse into the hard facts of governance. After all, as my father said, we are denizens of the earth. This is not jannat, paradise. It sobered me up.

Two days later

I wish this important event had not happened in the cold weather. I don't know...maybe summer might have been worse. Ammi has been preparing me for the change since my twelfth birthday. I recall how she had said, 'Mehru, jaan, you have to adopt the veil now that you're entering womanhood.'

'O Ammi!' I had protested.

'It is the custom,' she had said sternly. 'You have no choice. Remember hayaa, modesty, is the most important thing for a woman.'

'Why do the men have the freedom to do whatever they want?' I practically stamped my feet.

'It is the law of nature,' she had sounded resigned.

It was galling, but I knew I would have to abide by the rules, even though it seemed unfair. At times I wasn't too sure that I really wanted to grow up. I had noticed how my body was changing, and was torn between the delight of wielding power—like one of those princesses who could control men with their charm and beauty—and the carefree life of childhood. But it seemed like a paradox at times: they could bend men to their will, but society dictated that they had to live confined within the zenana.

Some of the emperor's wives and concubines hardly ever see him. They have their own mahals or apartments within the fort, lavishly furnished, a generous salary, all the jewels and clothes they can possibly wear, maids and servants at their beck and call. But they are also surrounded by the women guards, the darogas. Formidable ladies, dressed in male costumes,

armed with bows and arrows and swords. They see to it that no outsider enters the harem and that the ladies behave themselves too. It is an extraordinary thing, how well the five thousand inhabitants of the harem—from the queens, princesses and aristocrats to the concubines, singers, dancers and maids are supervised!

But till that thing happened, I didn't take growing up very seriously. Even before Ammi and Dilbagh warned me not to be scared when I began to bleed, I had known that all women had to suffer this way. My friend in court, Zameera, had started long before me. So, I was not so scared when it actually happened.

Immediately, I went and told Ammi. 'Allah be praised,' she raised her hands in prayer. 'I was beginning to get worried.' She held me close and sent for Dilbagh right away. After the old woman had helped me change, with much clucking and finger kissing, Ammi said, 'Child, there is much you need to know. I had decided to wait till it actually happened to inform you. Eh, Dilbagh bi, ask Aslam to make kheer and halwa. Each and everyone in the house must have some.'

'Ammi, does everyone have to know?' I cried.

'Mehru jaan, you have finally become a woman. This is an event to be celebrated.'

I couldn't help blushing when all the maids streamed in to congratulate me, receiving a bakshish of silver coins from Ammi.

But my back was aching and my stomach cramping so badly that I wanted to lie down. I didn't tell anyone, but Dilbagh knew. She led me away, quiet for once.

'My dear, while you are in this condition, you cannot offer your prayers,' Ammi said gently, later. 'Only on the fourth day, after washing your hair can you resume your religious duties. During the rozas you will have to abstain from fasting on these days. And...never, *never* take the risk of being alone with a man...'

I suppressed a shudder. It was bad enough that it was being made into a public announcement but the thought that I would be marked out during those days of the month disturbed me even more. Even my brothers and my father would know. How embarrassing!

A month later—November

I don't know why this cold and gloomy month was chosen for my brother Muhammad's wedding, but as Ammi explained, the bride's parents did not want to delay the nikah any further.

What would she be like, my sister-in-law? Would she be as affectionate as Saliha was? The thought of having the company of a girl closer in age to me than Khadija and Manija was exciting. My older sister visited us occasionally. I bombarded her with questions, eager to know what was going on in her life. She would reply with mundane things like choosing fabric for a new outfit for her husband's younger sister or going on an excursion with the family ladies. Honestly!

A large number of gifts arrived. Aziza's family were eager to please us it seemed. And then, like a dream it was all over. The feasting, the celebration, the rituals.

Two weeks later

I had barely begun to make friends with Aziza when the news came that Muhammad Sharif had received an appointment at court. I knew that my father was keen that my brother have an income of his own once he got married but I didn't expect it to happen so soon.

They left just yesterday, though my mother would have liked the new bride to spend more time with us. But my father said, 'It's best that she accompanies her husband. They have to set up house. Luckily, her parents are there in Lahore to offer support.'

A few days later—December

It snowed today! What a thrilling sight it was, when I first saw snow last year. I had imagined it would be like balls of cotton and it took me a few minutes to realize what the white powder drifting down from the sky was. Only when Shahpur and my two younger sisters came to drag me out, did it hit me. It was already beginning to settle on the grey stones of our courtyard. Manija was jumping up and down

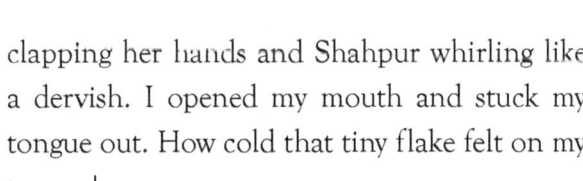

clapping her hands and Shahpur whirling like a dervish. I opened my mouth and stuck my tongue out. How cold that tiny flake felt on my tongue!

I don't know how long our antics would have continued had Dilbagh not screamed at us to come back inside. We dragged our feet in reluctantly. By then our clothes were quite damp and Khadija, who has always been quite delicate, was sneezing.

'You should have known better than to encourage the children,' Ammi sounded quite annoyed. 'Act your age, Mehru.'

'Ammi, it is the first time we have seen snow!' I had protested. But I accepted the bowl of hot kahwa, which Dilbagh bi pressed into my hands, gratefully.

We have become quite fond of this Kashmiri tea, though it's barely a year since the territory came under Mughal rule. The emperor loves the place, they say. It is even more beautiful than Kabul.

The next day

It's hard to believe that we have been here for one and a half years almost.

The news is that Salim is getting married again. Some Hindu raja has offered his daughter to him. Sometimes I wonder what his previous wives feel each time he remarries. Especially Jagat Gosaini. She's haughty, that one! His older begum, Man bai or Mariam-uz-Zamani as she has been named, is different. But they are princesses, their fathers have many wives and concubines too. All the same, don't they see each new wife as a potential challenger to their influence over Salim?

I would, if I were in their place...if...

The rumours are that he has begun to drink too much and take opium as well. There are also whispers about his disagreement with his father and his ambition to mount the throne. The Emperor has been very sick, poisoned some say. If it hadn't been for a Hindu vaidya, things would have gone badly. Baba was beside himself with anxiety, because the Emperor has been such a great benefactor to us. My father's livelihood and our well-being, all depends on his good will. At the Mughal court, fortunes can change at the speed of a lightning flash, we well know. Today a prince, tomorrow a beggar, Baba often says. Worse still, a prisoner. Wasn't Akbar's own father Humayun compelled to flee the country when he lost to Sher Shah Suri at the battle of Chausa and seek shelter in Persia?

With so many individual ambitions rubbing against each other, there is no dearth of men who would instigate the prince against his father to promote their own interests.

My heart melts at any mention of Salim. But is it right, I cannot help wondering, for a son to plot against his father? The Emperor who has been so good to us. 'Perhaps I'm better off here in Kabul,' Baba sometimes says. 'My own master, far from the intrigues of court.'

But from the eagerness with which he questions visitors from Lahore, I can see that he longs to return. Real influence and progress is possible only at the centre of the empire. If you are out of the emperor's sight, how can you impress him with the scope of your abilities?

Kabul is no doubt very important for Padshah Akbar. He had had a long conflict with his brother Mirza Muhammad Hakim over it, our tutor informed us. This was one of the reasons why he shifted his capital to Lahore—so that he could be closer to the western part of his empire. When he had driven his brother out, he had made his sister, Bakht-un-Nisa Begum, the governor.

I decided to paint a picture of this important sister of the Emperor. She must have been a strong lady. 'She had her brother's powerful support,' says our tutor in a matter-of-fact manner. 'Later the Padshah allowed his brother to return. But the sister remained in charge.'

What would I do if I were the governor of this province? The very thought makes me breathless. To be enthroned in a splendid court—even if it is behind a veil—with supplicants bowing to the ground before me. To issue commands that men rush to obey. To be responsible for the fate of thousands. To possess power over the life and death of any human being in this territory...

From an almost nobody, I would be someone

whose name was on everyone's lips. Poets would write verses addressed to me, favour seekers would besiege me with gifts. If I raised my voice even slightly, my subordinates would shiver.

Truly governors are very important, but it is the emperor before whom even governors tremble. Could a woman become an emperor or an empress, rather? Razia Sultana wielded immense power. There have been other important queens. And the Padshah Begum can bend the Emperor to her will if she pleases.

I think...I could do justice to such a position...

The Thirty Fifth Year of the Reign of His Majesty Abul Fath Jalal-Ud-Din Akbar

Kabul, January 1591

THIS RAINY, GLOOMY WEATHER can really wear you out. Our outdoor excursions have been severely curtailed. Much as I love them, Khadija and Manija get on my nerves with their squabbling. It is a good thing that Baba and Ammi have fixed such a strict routine for all of us and our house is large enough that one can retreat into a quiet corner.

I have begun to read Firdausi's *Shahnama*, the most important classic of Persian literature.

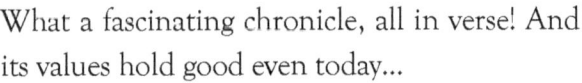

What a fascinating chronicle, all in verse! And its values hold good even today...

'Baba, do you ever miss your native land? Do you ever wish you could have stayed back in Persia?' I couldn't help asking my father one day.

He smiled, a little sadly, I think. 'Mehru jaan, the land of my birth is in my blood. It will always be part of me. But Hind is the land of my destiny. Nostalgia is like opium. If you overindulge in it, it will deaden your brain.' He became quite serious when he said this. 'A man who strives to excel in this world must grasp its reality, not wander in a world of dreams.'

The word opium sparked off a new train of thought in my head. My curiosity was so great that it squashed the slight hesitation I might have had in posing the question that sprang to my lips. 'Baba,' I whispered, 'is it true that Prince Salim has become a slave to opium?'

Baba started slightly. His eyes probed my face. 'Where did you hear this? Was it from Abul?'

The blood rushed to my face. I could not lie to my father but I didn't want to betray my beloved

older brother. 'I-I overheard a conversation,' I stammered.

Baba smiled thinly. 'It is true,' he said. 'It is an unfortunate thing. But there are people who would prefer to see a prince in the grip of an addiction so that they may be able to manipulate him to their own ends.' He shook his head. 'It is a great pity that the Mughal system pits father against son, brother against brother.' He sighed deeply.

For some reason, a wave of sorrow swept over me. Baba took my face between his hands. 'My child,' he said in a husky voice, 'our world abounds in rumours. Do not hesitate to ask me anything and I will inform you to the best of my ability. A girl of your intelligence should stay well informed of the ways of the Mughal court. Who knows when such knowledge might be of help?'

I flushed with joy. Any praise from my father makes me float on air.

Two weeks later—February

I haven't written anything about my friend Kauser Fatima, so far. I met her just a few months ago. Her mother Zohra Begum is the wife of one of the local aristocrats and would come to call on my mother quite often.

One day, as they sipped tea together, Ammi asked her, 'Zohra Begum, you once mentioned that you have a young daughter almost the same age as Mehr-un-nissa. Why don't you bring her over? Mehru needs the company of girls her own age.'

Zohra Begum smiled. 'I was wondering when you would ask me.'

She brought Kauser along the very next day. While we exchanged polite salaams, I noticed that she was much taller than me and had broader shoulders, which gave her an imposing appearance. Her large eyes were as brilliantly green as mine were blue. Though she spoke Persian—instead of the Turkish which is the language of the Mughal court—her accent was a little different from mine. (I must mention that I am fluent in both languages, as well as Arabic, though my parents say that it took them some time to master Turki when they first came here.) Could Kauser and I be friends?

'What would you like to do?' I asked her, like a well-mannered hostess. 'Shall we play chess or would you like to take a look at my latest piece of embroidery?'

'Can't we just talk?' she said, showing her pearly teeth in a broad smile. Her voice was deep and warm.

'Why not?' I replied, relieved that she sounded so friendly. It was a long time since I had the opportunity to indulge in idle chatter with a girl my age. 'Let's just talk.'

Talk turned out to mean gossip. After we had exchanged some vague conversation about our families and interests, as we nibbled on pine nuts, dried apricots and mulberries, I discovered that she was insatiably curious about life at the Mughal court: what the Mughal princesses liked to eat and wear and funnily enough, what did they fight over!

'I have heard that the Padshah's wives are always scheming to poison each other or their sons. That they trust their eunuchs more than their own mothers.' Her eyes became as large as saucers when she said that.

I couldn't help laughing. There was some truth in what she said. However, I felt a little uncomfortable divulging the details of the private lives of the Mughal princesses. Having been part of the inner circle, it felt like betrayal.

'Have you actually met the Padshah Begum?' Kauser asked.

My desire to boast overcame me then. 'Met?' I said, with a laugh. 'She is extremely fond of me and keeps calling me to court. She is a very kind lady. But if anyone angers her, then they're in serious trouble.'

'But how is it that the Mughal Emperor and the princes have married so many kafir women?' she wrinkled her nose.

'It is all politics,' I said grandly. 'The kafirs want the Emperor and his sons to marry their daughters so they remain friends and allies. And...and for the Emperor it is better to have allies rather than enemies.'

'But they say that the Emperor actually allows idol worship in his palaces,' she whispered, glancing around her in case someone might be listening. 'And that he has begun to follow a

new religion. People say he is no longer a true Muslim.'

Looking at the outrage obvious on her face, a malicious desire to shock her overcame me. A fleeting memory of the pujas that the Emperor was said to participate in, the havans his Rajput begums performed regularly flashed through my mind. The festivals too—like the Holi celebrations at court: all the princesses and their attendants dressed in white, spraying each other with colour; the musicians playing on their dholaks and the singing and dancing. And of course, the lavish festivities at Dusshera and Diwali.

'He is the Emperor of all Hindustan. He can do whatever he likes.' I shrugged. 'In fact, Padshah Akbar believes that all religions have some good qualities. He has espoused the cause of Sulah-i-kul or universal peace and begun a new religion called Tawhid-i-ilahi. It has the elements of several religions. However, he does not force it on anyone. He has so much respect for some Jain priests that he has given up eating meat and does not allow animals to be slaughtered on certain days.'

'Tauba-tauba!' Kauser touched her ears. 'I cannot believe that a true Mussalman can think of such things.'

I had heard such talk earlier. But it shocked me that a girl of my age had such a closed mind. I consider myself quite religious. I offer namaz five times a day, observe all my other religious duties. However, I could not bring myself to find fault with our Emperor's liberal beliefs.

'Sahiba, I do not think it is wise to speak thus of the Emperor,' I said severely. 'Let us concern ourselves with matters appropriate to our age.'

Kauser flung me a surprisingly sly glance from beneath her thick eyelashes. She smiled knowingly. 'Of course! This is talk for the mullahs not us. So, are you betrothed already?'

'Betrothed? No, my older sister and brother got married recently,' I replied. 'And I have another older brother. Are you?'

She flushed slightly and examined her hennaed finger nails. 'I was, a year ago.'

'Mubarak ho!' I leaned forward to embrace her. She smelt strongly of musk. 'But a year is a long time. Why are they delaying your marriage?'

She looked so downcast that I felt sorry I had asked. 'My mother-in-law keeps putting it off on some pretext or the other.' Then her face suddenly brightened. Deep dimples appeared in her cheeks as she smiled. 'But my fiancé says he can't wait. He-he writes to me secretly.'

'Oh...you lucky girl!' A wave of envy swept over me and a wrenching ache twisted my heart. If only someone—if Salim would write love letters to me, I would have been transported to the seventh heaven. 'What does he write?' I found it impossible to control my curiosity.

'That's a secret!' she said with a teasing smile. Then she suddenly looked worried. 'But please, please don't tell anyone. Swear on my head!'

'Only if you let me read one of the letters.' I picked up a chilgoza and cracked it between my teeth.

She clicked her tongue disapprovingly. 'You look so decorous. I never thought you would bargain for my secrets. All right, only one. Now promise.'

'On my own head.' I tried to look very serious. 'Remember to bring one the next time we meet.'

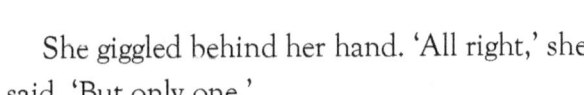

She giggled behind her hand. 'All right,' she said. 'But only one.'

Just a week later

How fortunate that I've found a friend to chatter with during these gloomy winter days. And a girl as lively as Kauser. She is surprised that Baba insists that all of us brothers and sisters receive the same kind of education. She exclaims over my embroidery, my paintings and my poetry.

After she showed me her precious love letter, we got the idea of composing a reply together. Her fiancé Ali Habibi seemed to be a real romantic. Without ever having seen her face, he was madly in love with her. He had written a poem describing himself as a lovelorn Majnu.

'If only I could send a befitting reply. But I have never written a poem in my life,' she said forlornly.

'I can help you,' I volunteered immediately. Till now I had written poems on the beauty of nature, or on philosophical and religious

themes. The idea of writing a love poem was absolutely thrilling.

We put our heads together and came up with the most lovesick verse ever.

> *Your words melt my heart*
> *like the snow on the mountains*
> *turns into water in the sun's heat.*
> *The rose bud of my heart longs to bloom*
> *Alas! the warmth of your breath remains*
> *distant.*

When we read out what we had written, Kauser jumped up and down, overcome with excitement. She hugged me so tight that I thought I would suffocate. She's a strong girl! Then she kissed the paper and said, 'If he doesn't force his mother to set a date now, I'll never get married.'

If only we could have guessed what repercussions the poem we composed so gleefully would have...

First of all, it set off such a heady train of

romantic thoughts in my mind that soon after Kauser left, I crept into a corner and dashed off a dozen more. How could I foresee that Abul would find them while shuffling through my compositions one day?

I have never seen such a furious look on his face! When he confronted me with that sheaf of paper in his hand, I immediately guessed what was going through his head.

Inwardly, I was shivering. But somehow, I steeled myself and tried to make light of it. 'Bhai jaan,' I said with a smile, 'those papers don't belong to you.'

My heart was thumping so loud that I was afraid he could hear it.

'They may not,' his tone slashed me like a knife, 'but as your brother, anything that pertains to the family honour concerns me. What is the meaning of all this?' he thundered. 'Who is this person?'

I thought quickly. If I told him the truth, my poor friend would be in hot water. 'Abul miyan, what are you saying? Is the Almighty a person?'

He had the grace to flush. '*Almighty?*' I have

never seen him look so embarrassed. 'Wh-what do you mean?'

I let out a tinkling laugh as I reached for the poems. 'Haven't we studied the immortal verses of the Sufi masters? I can't believe that you imagined that these verses were addressed to a man. That your sister has taken a lover.'

Sometimes it is good to take the bull by the horns. He turned a deep maroon and hung his head sheepishly. 'I forgive you this time,' I smiled. 'But just think about it. Had we been in Lahore or Agra, I would not blame you for being suspicious. But here? I live completely in purdah.'

He sighed deeply. 'You gave me a fright, Mehru,' he said. 'But please refrain from writing such verses. If they were to fall into the wrong hands, I shudder to think of the consequences.'

I grabbed the papers from him.

The next evening

If you had been a girl, dear roznamcha, you would have understood how painfully my heart was thumping at that moment. Worse, I heard

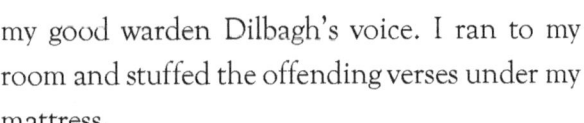

my good warden Dilbagh's voice. I ran to my room and stuffed the offending verses under my mattress.

When I went for my morning ride with Abul today, he still looked thoughtful.

'Did you ever actually meet Prince Salim?' he asked.

'Ammi and I met him once at the Meena Bazaar,' I said, wrinkling my brow.

'Hmmm,' he nodded. 'And what did he say?'

'Say? We both performed a low kornish. Ammi had mentioned it that evening.' I narrowed my eyes at him. 'Why are you asking suddenly?'

'No reason.' He shook his head. 'Those verses—they-they were quite different from your usual ones.'

'Bhai jaan!' I yelled. 'You're still suspicious. Isn't my word enough?'

'Calm down!' he hissed, looking around him nervously. 'You must understand that we need to be careful about your reputation. Just yesterday someone told me that Ali Habibi had broken his engagement. That girl is your friend, isn't she?'

'Kauser? No!' My stomach plunged sickeningly. 'But why?'

'Because she wrote lovelorn verses to him and he felt it was immodest.' His face was grim.

'It's not true! You're joking!' I almost fell off my horse in shock.

'Mehru jaan, why would I make up such stories?' he looked quite offended.

I was so overcome with rage that the only thing I could do was whip my poor horse into a gallop. Immodest? Just because she replied to his letters in kind? Arggh…I would have liked to strangle that stupid man!

Three days later

The weather is improving, but not my spirits. I used to eagerly await the festival of Nauroze in March. The Emperor celebrated it lavishly, even though it was a Shia festival. It would be an eighteen-day affair.

I had insisted to my mother that we go and meet Kauser, hoping against hope that the rumours were wrong.

The moment we entered the zenana, the

atmosphere of gloom that hung over the house dragged me down. The servant who let us in was subdued. She did not welcome us with smiles and flowery words as she usually did. We had to wait for a while before Kauser's mother entered, wrapping her shawl around her with shaky hands. Her smile was stiff and uncertain. When my mother drew her into a tight embrace, her shoulders shook with sobs.

'Is this true, what I'm hearing?' Ammi asked in hushed voice. 'Pray Allah, it's all a rumour.'

Zohra Begum twisted her hands and stared at the ground. She drew a deep breath, 'Sadly it is,' she murmured. 'Our Kauser's engagement has broken.'

I must have gasped aloud because she looked at me and said with a wan smile: 'I'm so glad you have come, Mehr,' she said. 'Your friend needs to be cheered up. She has barely eaten anything for the last few days.'

Kauser wouldn't look up or speak when I entered her room. I could see that she had flung on whatever clothes came to hand—she,

who was so particular. When I embraced her, the rank odour of sweat made my nostrils curl.

'Kauser...' was all I could say. She burst into tears. A strong feeling of guilt overcame me, as I wept along with her.

'It's all my fault,' I said. 'Can you ever forgive me?'

'No...it's my kismet,' she sobbed. 'I was the one who told you I wanted to write him a poem in reply.'

'It's so unfair,' I raged. 'He can write poems but you can't.' I drew a deep breath. 'This would not happen in the Mughal court.'

'This is Kabul,' she sighed. 'Women can't do all those things permissible in the Mughal court.' The severe note in her voice irritated me, despite my heartfelt sympathy.

Another week later

It is the festival of Nauroze and the gardens of Kabul have begun to bloom. When I looked out of my window this morning the sight of apples, pears and peach trees laden with pink and

white blossom, the multi-hued tulips and sweet-scented narcissus carpeting the ground, sent a wave of inspiration through my head. I had hurriedly begun to sketch out some embroidery designs when Dilbagh announced that Kauser and her mother had come to visit us.

My heart leapt with joy to see smiles on their faces again!

We learned that they had found another match for her. A much older man, and she will be his second wife. I didn't know whether to congratulate her...

'All this romance stuff is nonsense,' Kauser said, when I took her aside into our favourite corner to get all the details. 'All that's important is to find a good man who will keep you in comfort.'

Her eyes were expressionless and she glanced away when I tried to meet her gaze. I felt my heart would break, but I quickly pulled myself together and embraced her saying, 'Hazaar baar mubarak...may Allah grant you great happiness.'

A tiny shiver went through her body. Her eyes were damp when we pulled away. I could feel the anger flaring up inside me in an uncontrollable wave.

Who had ordained that women couldn't write love poems? I wished I were a man so that I could horsewhip Ali Habibi and make him cry for mercy.

But I said instead, 'Has the date been fixed? I want to embroider a special veil for you...in your favourite colour...emerald green.'

The smile reached her eyes at last. 'Will you? I will always treasure it as a memory of our friendship. Who knows how long you will remain here...'

'Long enough to attend your wedding, I'm sure, and-and even after that...' I trailed off lamely, because a feeling of guilt was sweeping over me. This whole business had burrowed such a deep hole in my heart that I wanted to flee Kabul right away. It felt like a curse to be a woman. What kind of world was this when the most innocent of acts can be turned against you?

But when she asked, 'The Emperor celebrates Nauroze? Surprising, considering it's a Shia

festival,' I knew she was recovering her spirits. I sent up a silent prayer.

'Oh yes! In great style. Didn't I tell you? Festivals of all religions are celebrated at the Mughal court.'

And when she pursed her mouth in that prissy way of hers, I almost burst out laughing. God willing, we would celebrate Nauroze in Lahore next year.

Ten days later

The skies are brilliantly blue and the mountains veiled in silver. The gardens are a riot of colour and maybe we will go for a picnic today.

Kauser is to be married next month. I have been so busy creating a garden on that gauzy silken veil for my friend, that my roznamcha has been sadly neglected. Will this fuchsia pink look good on emerald green? Or should I use a paler shade? Sometimes I regret my choice. A plain cream dupatta would have been the best. Personally, I prefer light shades, and for me there's no colour like pure, pristine white. If I had my way, even our fabulous carpets would be covered with white sheets. But emerald green is my friend's favourite and I do want to leave her with a memento that feels special, something she will always treasure.

My mother is my best adviser; when it comes to choosing shades of embroidery silk, I should consult her. Some spangles would add the shimmer that would make this special. My little sisters are of no use, though Khadija seems to be becoming a little more serious now. Even as I pull thread expertly through the fine fabric and watch the rose creeper bloom upon it, a thought won't leave my mind: *Revenge on Ali Habibi.*

Those poems disgust me now. Yesterday, I had pulled out that sheaf of paper and was wondering whether to tear the poems to bits or fling them into the fire, when Abul unexpectedly entered the room. He narrowed his eyes, probably noticing my sullen expression. He didn't speak for a moment, then he said, 'Don't destroy them. They are some of your finest.'

I gasped. 'How did you know I was going to destroy them?'

His mouth twitched. 'My dear sister, don't I remember this expression from the time when you hurled a pot of water on the ground and smashed it, just because Ammi hadn't allowed you to go out and play?'

I flung the papers down, clicking my tongue angrily. 'They are ill omened. If only I could...' I bit my tongue to stop the words from gushing out.

'If only...what?' Abul turned wary. 'Why ill omened?'

I had to tell him. 'I-I helped to compose the poem that broke Kauser's engagement...'

He was silent for a moment. 'I knew it,' he said quietly.

'If only I could horsewhip that lout!' I fumed. 'Why did he send her poems if he didn't want any response to them?'

'He's a fool,' Abul grimaced. 'Forget it, Mehru...'

'But he broke her heart...and somewhere I feel responsible because I wrote them for her.' I was almost in tears.

Abul put a comforting hand on my

shoulder. 'Will it make you feel better if he's horsewhipped?'

'It'll be like a soothing balm on an aching wound.' I definitely meant what I said.

'All right, I'll arrange for it,' Abul said.

'Abul...you won't do it yourself?' My hand flew to my heart.

'It is easy to hire men for the purpose,' Abul shrugged.

'But I will pay,' I insisted.

'As you wish, sister dear.' Abul stroked his glossy beard and smiled.

A few days later

I had wasted no time in running to my room and opening up my chest. A considerable cache had accumulated there—silver rupiyas and even some gold coins which I had received as gifts on festivals. From my parents and relatives mostly, the Empress was very open handed too and her soft corner for me ensured that she gave generously. There never seemed much of an opportunity to spend it here. There were no Meena Bazaars, like at the court.

'That's enough,' Abul said, when I poured five mohurs into his palm. 'They will happily finish him off for less.'

'Please, Abul...' I put my palm on his mouth. Suddenly I felt nervous. Did I want a man's blood on my conscience?

'I'll tell them to make sure he's bedridden for a couple of months at least,' Abul's black eyes gleamed merrily.

I couldn't help giggling at the thought. 'I wish I could have his mother beaten up too!' I exclaimed.

'You are becoming more and more bloodthirsty, sister!' Abul laughed aloud. 'I will have to be very careful around you.'

'Yes, you better!' I thumped his back hard.

'Hai! I'm not Ali Habibi, Mehru!' he pretended to groan.

A week later

Just a couple of weeks left for Kauser's nikah. I am furiously at work finishing the veil.

Ammi and I have been visiting them regularly to help out with the preparations. Zohra Begum is so much in awe of my mother's expertise that it's funny at times.

'Asmat apa, this is the menu we have made for the wedding feast,' she will say with a nervous flutter of her hands. 'Do you approve?'

'Let me see.' Ammi also likes to feel important, I can sense. Who wouldn't?

We check out Kauser's trousseau: silk and velvet shalwars, gold-embroidered peshwaz, heavy necklaces of gold studded with precious stones, a variety of shawls. She seems content. Her bridegroom, though grey-haired, is a big landowner. He has four children from his first wife, but only one son. Apparently, he's quite eager to add to his brood. I examine the jewelled dagger that will be one of the gifts. Will my parents present such gifts to my intended? But the person I dream of marrying has an excess of such goods. Suddenly, I feel uneasy. Are my ambitions pitched too high?

The flower I was embroidering with such tiny stitches was just about complete, when I sensed a presence. Upon looking up, I noticed that it was Dilbagh, with that particular look on

her face—the look she has when she's bursting to unload some sensational news.

I felt a little irritated, though my skin went taut, sensing what it could possibly be. I wanted to know and yet not know. When I continued to concentrate on my embroidery, she prowled around the room, picking up a discarded garment to fold, or just shift something around till I wanted to scream.

Finally, I said, through tight lips, 'So...what is it?'

'What?' she raised her scanty eyebrows innocently.

'Come on, Dilbagh bi, this is not the time of the day when you tidy up my room. Out with it!' I bit off the end of the thread viciously.

'All right...' she said. 'I thought this might please you. You've been in a foul mood ever since your friend's engagement was broken... even though you try not to show it...'

'Dilbagh...' There was a warning note in my voice but she ignored it.

Her voice went down to a whisper, 'I've heard that a group of men set upon Ali Habibi

last night and whipped him unconscious. No one knows who they were and why they did it. If a passer-by hadn't come along, who knows what might have happened...'

I faced her squarely though my insides were roiling like a butter churn. 'Interesting...' I said. 'He should not have been roaming around the streets alone at night. This city is full of robbers and other hooligans. I'm surprised he was.'

She threw an unbelieving glance at me, and left shaking her head.

I hugged myself with delight when I was sure she was far away. Then my eyes spilled over. Something began to stir in my heart. It would be poetic justice to mark the event with a verse.

> *Heartless one, you trampled*
> *the perfumed bouquet I offered*
> *in the dust, not knowing*
> *that even the powerless can give back*
> *pain for pain.*
> *Revenge is sweet, my love.*

Ten days later

It is three days since Kauser's nikah took place. I felt strangely numb throughout the wedding celebrations. Her husband also lives in Kabul, so I would have no problem visiting her there, but I knew I never would. It was already beginning to feel that our friendship was a closed chapter.

It was Kauser who had begun to withdraw. When I went to meet her just a couple of days before the festivities began, she hardly spoke at all. In fact, she pleaded a headache and said she wanted to lie down. I had brought my gift, the gauzy emerald green veil I had embroidered with such love. Everyone who set eyes on it had burst into praise. But she did not even open the gold-embroidered velvet case in which I had placed it. Our embrace was stiff and awkward. I should have felt hurt, but for some strange reason I was not.

'She is nervous no doubt,' Ammi said understandingly.

Kauser's mother nodded and brushed at her eyes. 'This is the fate all girls are born to. Ahh...' she let out a painful sigh. Then she touched my

cheek and kissed her hands. 'Do not mind, my child, you have been such dear friends. When the day comes for your departure from your parents' home, you will understand what our little Bulbul is going through.'

I am not one for such gestures, but I spontaneously reached out to squeeze her hand. 'How can I mind, Khala,' I said. 'We have been like sisters...I hope she likes my gift.'

Soon after we rose to leave. I could not help wondering if Kauser had heard about the attack on Ali Habibi. Of course, she had! But could she have connected me with it? Very likely!

A few days later—23 May

In a week's time, I will turn fourteen. Another year has gone by. I have grown a little more during the past year, but Dilbagh says I have reached my full height. I am getting a little fed up of weddings, I must admit. I have attended so many during the past year. It's nice to dress up, of course. Ammi had let me borrow some of her jewellery for Kauser's wedding. I loved the studded jhumkis. The rubies went so well with my deep crimson shalwar. Since the weather has turned warmer, I wore a velvet choli with a fine white muslin jama on top. Ammi's pearl necklaces glowed softly on my well-developed bosom. As I preened at myself in the mirror before we left, I couldn't help thinking...must say, I look a real woman now.

'Asmat Begum, are you looking for a match for her in Kabul?' an old crone had squawked, as we offered polite salaams to the other women.

A wave of disgust soured my mouth. Was this all they could talk about? Ammi smoothly replied: 'Ah...Samia Begum...first I want to get done with welcoming Abul's bride into the household. Then it will be Mehr-un-nisa's turn.'

'Try this almond and saffron sweet,' a woman with dense eyebrows said. Then she looked at me slyly. 'You will have no problem finding a match for this blue-eyed beauty. Is your daughter-in-law also of Persian birth?'

'Indeed, she is,' Ammi's chin rose up. 'Her father is from a family equal to us in status.'

'You will miss your friend,' a kindly lady dressed in a splendid purple outfit smiled at me. Her pearls seemed even larger than ours.

'Who knows how much longer we will stay here? The Emperor can call us back any moment,' Ammi shrugged. 'And then, she has her sisters for company.'

The dense-eyebrowed woman whispered, 'Did you hear about the attack on Ali Habibi? They say that he is still bedridden.'

My cheeks felt hot and I hoped no one had noticed me flushing. I chewed some sugared almonds furiously. Old women! They have nothing else to do but gossip.

Ten days later

Yes, I said that I'm sick of weddings. But how can I not feel happy for my dear brother? Abul's beard has a special gloss to it these days, it seems. He cannot stop smiling.

Among the various gifts he received from his in-laws was a splendid Arab horse. We still go out riding together in the mornings and I practise with my rifle.

'Diwanji-Diwanji, that is all my heart sings,' I cried out today, as we jogged along.

Diwanji is the name of his betrothed. But my

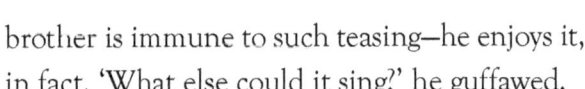

brother is immune to such teasing—he enjoys it, in fact. 'What else could it sing?' he guffawed.

'Does she know everything that's in your heart?'

'She will. What is a wife for?' Nothing could ruffle his composure.

I laughed wholeheartedly. My heart was bursting with pride at this intelligent, handsome brother of mine. We were the most talented family around, I sometimes felt. Hadn't my father already demonstrated it with his brilliant managing of the Emperor's finances?

And we, his children, would prove it in times to come.

A faint drizzle began to fog the air before us. I put up my face to feel it on my cheeks. Cool and fresh...

'Let's see how fast your Arab steed can gallop,' I called, spurring my horse.

Abul outraced me that day. Of course, he had the advantage of having a better horse than mine. I laughed to see him wiggle his thumb at me in triumph.

'Never mind, bhai jaan,' I said. 'Today you win, next time it might be my turn.'

'Keep hoping,' he said. 'You will never win against me.'

'Let's see,' I shrugged. 'There are many kinds of races.'

'Ah...I can see you are an ambitious girl,' he grinned. 'Let's see how high you can fly on your dreams.'

'Far into the sky, bhai jaan,' I smiled sweetly.

Abul shrugged. But I believed in the power of my dreams.

A few days later

I should be more regular with my roznamcha. Maybe when I am older I might be interested in looking back and recalling how we spent our days in this remote part of the empire. My first roza is definitely something I would like to recall. Yes, this year I am fasting, since I am considered old enough now.

Our routine has changed a great deal during this holy month of Ramzan. My parents are particular about the laws of religious observances. I remember when I was nine, I once asked my father if I could observe the fast, and he had said, 'There is a proper time for everything.' I was a little disappointed because some parents allowed younger children to observe the rozas. Now I understand better why certain rules have been made.

We rise in the early hours of the morning for our seheri, the repast that will carry us through the day. It feels strange to be up and about while it is still so dark. For some reason, we speak in hushed tones. The men have been up late into the night, attending the tasweeh, the readings from the Quran in the mosque. We had gone too, in the afternoon to pray in the women's section.

The whole family gathers to listen to Baba reading from the Quran. Then Dilbagh lays out the meal along with her helpers. There are the nuts and dried fruits that Kabul is famous for, but I prefer the fresh apricots and peaches to begin the meal. A rich soup of trotters, succulent kebabs and a hearty lamb stew will follow along

with naan. We will end with some halwa and a yogurt drink. The first day Ammi warned me to eat slowly. I have never been a big eater, but the thought of not having any food through the day made me stuff myself. And actually, my appetite has grown ever since we came here. Whether it's the mountain air or the fact that I'm gaining height, it's hard to say.

I hate to admit it, hate to admit my weakness, but the first day was tough. I felt drained and sluggish. Luckily, my body adjusted after two or three days. This is a time for reading the Quran and giving to the poor, my father said, for disciplining your body and soul.

After the fajr prayers are over, we try to maintain our routine. The tutor comes for our lessons and we lose ourselves in the study of literature and history, astronomy and mathematics.

In the afternoon, apart from Baba and Abul, most of us rest. Khadija, Manija and Shahpur, of course, carry on with their usual antics. Yesterday, I had dozed off when my two younger sisters burst into my room asking me

to resolve a quarrel. I jumped up, ready to give them a firing.

Then the terrified looks on their faces lashed me like a splash of cold spring water. Baba always says, 'Mehru, try to control your temper. You have every good quality possible, except that you are quick to anger.' I recalled that this is the month we are supposed to practise gentle behaviour and swallowed the harsh words that were rising to my lips. However, by then they had run away.

When the call of the muezzin announces the end of the fast, the whole city seems to spring into life. We feed each other with dates as we gather around the dastarkhwan laid out, take deep sips of rose flavoured sherbet, tuck into the lamb pilau and kofte. I have always felt the local style of cooking is a little insipid. Abul agrees. We are used to the fragrant spices and creamy gravies of the Mughal court. But our cooks have travelled with us from Lahore and know our taste. Only when we are invited for an ifftar meal by a local grandee do our tongues cry out for richer flavours.

Every day our parents distribute food to the poor, along with money. The first evening Ammi suggested that we take a round of the city to get a glimpse of the festivities. My heart thudded with a sudden excitement as I climbed into the silk-lined palanquin. Last year too, we had toured Kabul a few times, but each sight and sound felt more vivid this year. The city was brilliantly lit—the mosques and the mansions of the rich were hung with festive lanterns and the sense of celebration was all pervasive. Kabul is a city to which many races of people throng—the native Afghans, fierce in their dense beards and huge plumed turbans; the Tajiks, a Persian speaking people who have a large population here; the Hazaras, said to be descendants of Changez Khan, with distinctly Mongolian features; Turks and Persians in their embroidered jamas with tall hats crowning their heads; to the weather-beaten Uzbeks with drooping moustaches, a group whom our Emperor abhors. The lively buzz of voices in the air was an indistinguishable welter of speeches and accents.

The display of food at the eating places made me goggle. Huge platters of dates, stacks of naan and sweets were arrayed on their counters, along with mounds of pilau and a vast variety of succulent meats. In fact, the delicious aroma of cooking food made me quite hungry again. Fascinated, I watched stout men energetically pulling out freshly roasted legs of lamb from tandoors, chickens and other grilled meats, piling them into plates for the waiting customers. Those who had already been served were chomping on the food with great relish.

'Shall we have that tomorrow?' Shahpur, who was riding alongside us on a pony, pointed to a whole sheep grilling over a fire. Glistening with fat, it had turned an appetizing reddish brown colour.

'You will have to eat it all!' Khadija giggled.

'Of course, I can!' he stuck out his chest proudly. He is already beginning to fancy himself as a little man. (He did look quite handsome in his deep blue velvet jama with a small dagger tucked into the band at his waist.)

At that moment, Ammi called out to the palanquin bearers to take us back. 'We will come again,' she said.

Suddenly, I felt ready to flop into bed.

A week later

As each day of the fast passed, I was congratulating myself that I was acquiring better control over myself. Today, however, I realized it is not that easy to suppress my angry impulses.

It was not entirely my fault. Why are my siblings so irritating? Manija and Khadija came dashing into my room as usual, but so wildly that they knocked over my inkpot. The poem I was writing was blotted out and some drops spattered my pale lemon peshwaz—a favourite one. I raised my hand to slap Khadija, who was the actual culprit, when she cheekily said, 'Apa, what are you doing? Remember what Baba said, about not hitting us during Ramzan?'

My hand dropped. But I couldn't help exclaiming, 'You little witch! That does not mean that you can come and destroy everything in my room. Not only have you ruined my poem but my dress as well. Don't ever enter my room again!'

The two left, hanging their heads. I felt a little sorry that I'd been so harsh but someone needs to discipline them. Luckily the words of my poem were still playing in my mind so after their maid Sana had cleaned up the place, I could write it down again.

My poems bring me the kind of peace that no one can imagine. The moment I sit down with my quill and a sheet of paper, I feel all my gloomy thoughts transform themselves into beautiful words and a peculiar calm descends on my heart. I read them aloud to myself. Sometimes I add a tune and sing them, accompanying myself on my rabab. The whole universe seems to be in harmony at such moments. The boredom of being shut up indoors when I would rather be riding up a steep mountain path, the ache of being so far away from Salim...worrying that we might never meet, vanishes. This world is full of woes, but poetry helps you to blot them out.

I decided to send this poem to the Padshah Begum in my next letter. She had actually sent

a note of congratulation on Abul's engagement when I wrote and informed her.

Where is she right now? Lahore, I suppose. Both Agra and Lahore are unbearably hot at this time. She must be spending most of her time soaking in a scented pool, with her maids bringing her glasses of cool sherbet or spicy aam panna. Some women will be working the huge pankhas, others splashing water on the khas curtains. Suddenly I feel nostalgic for the fragrance of this wonderful root. Garlands of bela and chameli would be adding their perfume. I can even imagine her feasting on succulent mangoes. How I love mangoes! We do manage to get them transported here, but in limited quantity. The luscious langda must be piling up in the mandis right now.

Three days later

This was our second Eid in Kabul. And it seemed as if the whole city had turned out to greet us. The cooks had been up from the early hours: roasting, boiling, stir frying. Ammi was up too, to supervise all the preparations. We had begun to decorate the house a day earlier. There is no shortage of flowers in this season, even roses are blooming here, so I could design all kinds of festive garlands.

We were rushed off our feet greeting guests in the zenana. I was being crumpled in the embrace of an older lady who could have vanquished a seasoned wrestler, when Ammi called out insistently, 'Mehr, Mehr, look who is here!' I made a grateful escape and when my eyes fell on Kauser, I cried out with joy and ran to hug her. She had probably not expected such an effusive welcome, so was a little awkward in the beginning.

'Mashallah! You're positively blooming!' My mother kissed her fingers and gently touched shoulders with my friend. When they drew back, I noticed the bulge that Kauser was trying to hide under her dupatta.

'Mubarak ho!' I whispered. For some reason, my eyelids stung. 'You are blooming, as Ammi says...'

She flushed and dropped her gaze. 'Come,' I drew her away to a corner before all the

congratulatory women could inundate us. 'How have you been? When is the baby due?' The questions flew thick and fast.

Dilbagh appeared with a glass of almond milk. 'Drink this, my child,' she said. 'You will need to keep up your strength.'

Both of us began to giggle helplessly. Time seemed to drop away as we chatted. It was almost like old times.

After the rush of visitors was over, we collapsed on to our takhts. Baba shrugged off his embroidered satin choga and took a long, grateful drag on his hookah. My feet were aching and I could not help wondering how Ammi held up so gracefully under this onslaught. Always smiling, always ready with a pleasant response to the most sharp-tongued woman. She was a real asset to my father. A wife's petulant words have been the downfall of many an ambitious courtier, I have heard—in the Emperor's zenana, of course. That is the place to acquire wisdom of all kinds and that is where many careers blossom or fade.

Khadija, Manija and Shahpur began to

pester Baba for their Eidi. He opened up his velvet pouch and began to distribute coins. 'Don't you want your Eidi, Mehru?' he smiled.

'When you're through with these brats,' I smiled back. Last year I had been out-clamouring them. This year, somehow, I felt it was too childish.

It had been a good day. Kauser's visit had made it more special. But nothing could compare with the Eid at Padshah Akbar's court. When would we return? Suddenly, I felt unhappy again.

'No brooding on this blessed day, dear sister.' It was Abul's light baritone voice.

'I'm not brooding,' I protested.

'I know that expression too well,' he grinned.

My dark mood vanished as we sparred...

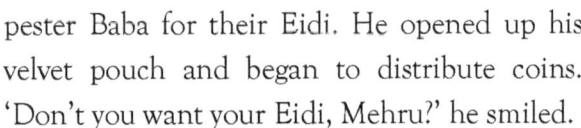

Three weeks later

It has happened! There is a new addition to our family: Abul's wife Diwanji. If I were the hero-worshipping type, I would be hanging around her like Khadija and Manija, admiring all her outfits and jewellery. Even Shahpur seems to have lost his heart to his new sister-in-law.

She is a pretty, sweet-tempered thing, I agree. And Abul obviously dotes on her. I am happy for my brother, though I miss our morning rides together. They have become somewhat irregular since he got married.

I have to admit that Abul's wedding was the most splendid one so far in my family. We travelled to Lahore for the mangni, the engagement. I was excited to be back at the court, but our visit was extremely short.

Every day, I send up a dua that we return to Lahore soon. It seems that only then will my life begin. Right now, it's as if I'm poised on the threshold of my destiny.

My routine continues—my prayers, breakfast, the tutor, the music lessons, my embroidery, poetry writing.

What our tutor told us yesterday about the history of this region really intrigued me. He told us that this area had been populated by Buddhists once and they had carved huge idols of the Buddha into the mountainside at a place called Bamiyan.

That night as I helped Baba with his

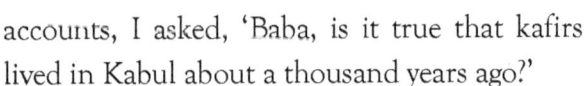

accounts, I asked, 'Baba, is it true that kafirs lived in Kabul about a thousand years ago?'

'Yes, my dear. As it was in Hindustan, this region did not see the light of Islam till true believers from the West spread the word,' my father nodded somewhat absently. I could see he was deeply preoccupied, but could not control my curiosity.

'They say that there are enormous idols carved into rocks at a place called Bamiyan. That they are over a hundred feet high. How could the kafirs manage such a feat so long ago?'

Baba smiled. 'My dear, in matters of religion they may not have seen the light, but the unbelievers had other forms of knowledge. Men who have seen them, talk about the enormous temples with intricately carved idols, decked with gold and jewels.'

'It seems almost unbelievable...but our tutor says that like in Hindustan, a very advanced civilization existed here in the past.' I tried to imagine a different way of life in this very place, hundreds of years ago.

'This is what travel to distant places does for us.' Baba put his quill back into the inkpot and scratched his beard. 'It widens our knowledge and shows us the kinds of possibilities that exist in this world.' Then he looked at me keenly. 'Would you like to see those idols for yourself? The weather will be tolerable for the next few months. Your brother's wedding is out of the way, and by now I think I have got a good handle over the finances of this province. Maybe it's time for a short trip.'

'Tauba, tauba, Baba! Why would I want to look at the idols of unbelievers?' I quickly put my hands on my ears.

'Child,' he looked at me thoughtfully, 'these are marvels of art and architecture. You have always shown much interest in finding out how buildings are constructed. Some of our rulers have indeed thought of destroying these statues, even tried to. But it's worth trying to find out the secrets of their creation.'

I smiled and embraced him. 'Baba, you are always wise and full of understanding. Let us discover the secrets of the infidels. Maybe one day we might be able to use that knowledge to our advantage.'

The thought of making that journey excited me so much that I had a hard time falling asleep that night.

A few days later

The weather has been somewhat rainy. But it is like that here. You never know when clouds will sweep over the mountains and the heavens open up. But it is not like the constant downpour you experience in Hindustan at this time of the year.

Our trip to Bamiyan has been planned for late August after Abul returns from Lahore. He is taking Diwanji for the customary visit to her parents. I am not sure if I am pleased that they will be gone. Sometimes I wish to return to the old times, before Abul was married and all his attention was not centred on one person. I know I sound like a jealous sister...but we have always been so close.

I suppose this is what growing up is about... changing relationships. The one above knows that I have tried to be as nice as I can to Diwanji.

I cannot fawn upon her like my little sisters—
that would be silly and childish. They run to
her with her favourite sweets and fruits and
constantly vie for her attention.

One day Dilbagh remarked, 'Soon it will be
your turn to enter another household. Pray to
Allah that they are as welcoming as your family
have been to Abul's Begum.'

'We'll see when the time comes,' I snapped,
unable to control my irritation. What was she
implying? Haven't I been as warm as I can to the
newcomer in our family?

'Child, you may be as lovely as a pari from
jannat, clever and accomplished in every way,
but in the end, it is your kismet that decides the
course of your existence.' She cast a disapproving
look at me. 'Fear God and be humble.'

I wanted to burst out saying, 'There is nothing
wrong with my kismet. Doesn't Baba always say
that I was his tabeez against misfortune?' But
something stopped me. What she said about
being humble...and then Dilbagh is like a family
member. Ammi always says that we should be
grateful to have a person as outspoken as her in

our household. She will always let us have the correct measure of every action. And that itself is the biggest protection against misfortune. Don't we hear, over and over again, of this powerful noble or that who fell from grace? Leave alone a dushazari mansabdar, even a wazir cannot feel he is secure. It may sound like treason, but even an emperor's crown may not stay on his head if fortune wills otherwise.

'You are right,' I replied as humbly as I could. 'If you fear God and do your duty, fortune will also favour you.'

She looked at me disbelievingly for a moment, then shook her head and left.

Two weeks later

How infuriating! Our trip was cancelled because Baba has been swamped with visitors from court. But Kauser has given birth to a baby boy! How exciting it was to visit her, after the customary days of seclusion were over. She is really blooming now. Her eyes are filled with a dreamy contentment and her smile is warm and melting. She has become quite fat though!

When I took the tiny, helpless creature
into my arms something melted inside me as I
inhaled his raw, milky scent.

'Careful! Watch his head,' Ammi said, but I
could barely hear her. His cheeks were so satiny
soft that I couldn't stop stroking them. I think I
will make a good mother, when the time comes.

The Thirty-Sixth Year of the Reign of His Majesty Padshah Abul Fath Jalal-Ud-Din Muhammad Akbar

1592

THIS IS THE WORST SEASON OF THE YEAR. Cold winds lash the city, water turns to ice in the open. Dilbagh is full of complaints about her numerous aches and pains. She is constantly brewing all kinds of healing potions. The only glimmer of hope on the horizon is that Baba says that there is a chance that we will return to court this year.

Two months later

At last it has come—the Emperor's summons! We are going back to Lahore. Baba showed me the farman with the royal seal on it. I am beside myself with excitement.

'Allah be praised,' Ammi had raised her hands up to the heavens. 'You have been able to fulfill your responsibilities here and keep the Emperor satisfied.'

Baba had followed suit, murmuring a quiet prayer. For a moment, it was as if a cold wind from the mountains had dampened my joy. How much we live in fear of the Emperor...I have heard about spies who keep constant watch on the officials. I wonder what it feels like to wield such immense power. I know none of the Mughal women have mounted the throne, unlike Razia Sultan or Rani Durgawati of Gondwana, whose heroism is legendary or Chand Bibi. They exert their influence in different ways. I have memories of Ruqayya Begum's peremptory commands and her loud interjections when the Emperor is holding court. His foster mothers Maham Anaga and

Jiji Anaga were able to bend him to their wishes too, I have heard.

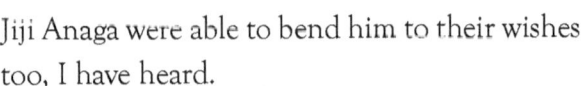

Two weeks later

Lahore at last! The last few days have been so busy that I haven't had time to scribble even a sentence. We arrived here after a journey that stretched over two weeks. How different it felt! How silly and childish I was when we had set out to Kabul! There is so much I have experienced there. Returning, I wished I could turn into a bird with huge wings and zoom back swiftly to Lahore.

The sun felt scorching hot, though it is still spring, dusty winds were flinging dry leaves through the streets. I was breathless with excitement as we passed through the gates into the city. Everything seemed so different from Kabul—the sights, the sounds, the smells...the people on the streets.

We had barely stepped into our house, and our luggage was being unloaded when Baba said, 'Asmat Begum, I must leave right away to pay my respects to the Emperor. Please find some suitable clothes for me.'

'Right away...' Ammi began, then fell silent. She turned to one of our manservants and asked him to fetch the chest that held Baba's clothes. Baba gulped down some sherbet and made a hasty meal, then mounted his horse and trotted off.

It was almost evening when he returned. We were still unpacking. My eyes popped out when I set eyes on my father. Baba was adorned with a robe of honour, he was bearing a jewelled sword which the Emperor had presented him! This was an achievement to be proud of.

'Ammi, bring out some sweets!' Abul called.

'Quickly!' Muhammad added his voice. Both my brothers had accompanied my father to the darbar.

'Mubarak! Hazaar bar mubarak!' Ammi was breathless with joy. But Baba's smile looked forced. A sharp fear pinched me. What was wrong?

Later, when I asked him, he opened up to me as he always does. 'Ah...child,' he sighed. 'The Emperor may sit on a golden throne but... his majesty has aged, his health is not so good.'

A hard fist clutched my heart. 'Oh Baba...but he has the best of hakims to attend to him...'

'That he does,' Baba said. His mouth twisted in a bitter smile. 'One of them attended to him too well.'

I shuddered, thinking of the rumours... that Salim, eager to mount the throne, had influenced the hakim to poison his father. Salim...who made me go weak in the knees. I wanted to weep.

'Allah grant our gracious Emperor a long life,' I said fervently.

'Indeed...and yes, Mehru...the Padshah Begum has ordered that you and your mother wait on her tomorrow.' His eyes softened, when he heard my gasp of excitement.

Three days later

I don't know how many outfits I must have changed that day. Finally, even my easy-going mother lost patience. 'Mehru! You are not dressing up for your wedding!' she cried.

'Going to court is like attending a wedding,' my sister-in-law Diwanji smiled. She's in the last stages of her pregnancy and moves with great difficulty, but was keen to help me get dressed. 'Why don't you try this ghaghara of mine? It's brand new and I will not be able to wear it for some time. The blue choli will go well with your eyes. You will outshine all the princesses.' She giggled.

I could not help hugging her.

A gauzy white dupatta spangled with silver draped over my head, and my mother's kundan choker gleaming at my throat, I felt positively regal as I stepped into the palanquin. Dilbagh made a sign against the evil eye as we left. But when we reached the palace, I felt I was in a daze. Then a cold spasm of fear gripped me. It had been such a long time...what kind of welcome would we receive? But the Empress had summoned us...the question hovering at the back of my mind was—would I catch a glimpse of Prince Salim?

It was a futile hope, but I saw his little son Khurram all right. After we had passed through the outer row of sentries—the Ahadis—then presented our credentials to the women guards who patrol the zenana, a eunuch ushered us inside. The Padshah Begum welcomed us warmly. As usual, she lay imperially inclined on her couch, her attending ladies and slave girls ranged around her. Her black velvet cap was ornamented with a huge sapphire surrounded by glittering diamonds and a small white feather. The brightness of her gold-sprigged crimson shalwar was muted under her gauzy, spangled jama. I blinked, I had forgotten how dazzling the jewels in her necklaces could be. She was puffing on a hookah. It seemed as if time had frozen, till I noticed the grey strands in her hair.

'Did you have a good stay in Kabul, Asmat Begum?' she asked my mother formally. 'And you, Mehr-un-nissa...you're a young woman now.' She looked me up and down and smiled crookedly. 'Hmmm...you have grown into a beauty. How old is she?' I felt my cheeks go hot at her scrutiny.

'Sixteen, your majesty,' my mother replied politely.

'It's time that you were married, my dear,' the Padshah Begum said in a peremptory tone.

My mother made a low bow. 'With your blessings, we hope she will be soon.'

Just then a maid entered, carrying a curly headed baby. 'My son!'said the Padshah Begum, beaming all over.

Later I learned that Ruqayya Begum had asked the Emperor to let her bring up Jagat Gosaini's son as her own, after an astrologer predicted he was destined for greatness. The proud Rajput princess had to agree. How she must have suffered, giving up her six-day-old baby! This— bringing up another royal lady's child—is, however, fairly common among the Mughals.

But I was glad that Diwanji lent me her ghaghra. The Rajput fashions are more popular in court now.

Ruqayya Begum told my mother to send me to attend on her every day. Definitely, one of these days I will set eyes on Salim. But will he know who I am?

A week later

Barely have we unpacked than the Emperor has decided to move to Agra. I feel sorry for my

sister-in-law. How uncomfortable it must be for her to be suspended on the back of a camel all day. But she is good natured about it.

27 April

Diwanji's pains began soon after we arrived in Agra. I must confess that I had been looking forward eagerly to returning to our childhood home. What good times we used to have there.

But Diwanji's groans and screams made me nervous. Why do women have to suffer so much to give birth?

At last the baby was born, a sweet little girl. And wonder of wonders, she has grey-blue eyes like me!

Swaddled tightly in a white cloth, she was made to lick honey from a silver spoon and the azaan was sounded in her ears. Baba had the privilege of naming Abul's daughter. He chose Arjumand Bano.

Two weeks later

What a delight it is to have a little baby in the house. Even my father loves to hold her in his arms.

But my birthday is arriving. I will complete sixteen now. I feel quite old. Many girls my age are married already. Didn't the Empress sound almost as if she was displeased with my unmarried state?

1 June 1593

The Emperor and the princes are weighed against twelve different items on their birthdays—ranging from gold, silk, perfumes, copper and salt to seven kinds of grains. All this is distributed to the poor. I have no reason to complain, though. As my mother says, we should give thanks to the almighty for the blessings that we enjoy.

In Kabul we led a quiet existence. After my lessons I would settle down to my embroidery or write some poetry. Here, we head out for the court. Yesterday, when I said my salaams to the Padshah Begum, she said, 'I have something for you...see, my spies are everywhere. I know it is your birthday.'

Everyone around her burst into laughter. I performed a deeper taslim and replied politely:

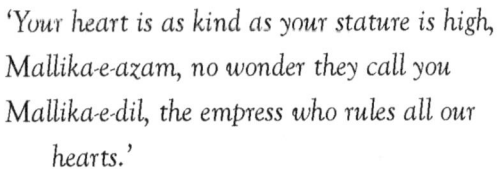

'Your heart is as kind as your stature is high, Mallika-e-azam, no wonder they call you Mallika-e-dil, the empress who rules all our hearts.'

The Empress's smile grew broader, 'Subhan Allah,' she cried, kissing her fingers. The ladies around her echoed her words. So did the eunuchs hovering close by. My heart swelled with pride. I wasn't sure how the poem had sprung out of my mouth. But I am always grateful for this gift because Ruqayya Begum delights in my talent for repartee.

'May you live long! Come here.' She embraced me warmly. 'You deserve a more lavish present than the one I have for you. Here!' She pulled off one of her rings and presented it to me. My head swam. It was a huge diamond.

I bent low to the ground, trying not to notice the envious looks in the other women's eyes.

Fortunately, my mother who had accompanied me, had brought a platter of sweets along with a nazar—a gift for the Empress. She began to offer them to everyone and the mood changed.

When Ruqayya Begum demanded that I set the poem to music, I asked for some time. Maybe by chance, Salim might be around when I was singing it.

Two weeks later

The ring is loose on my finger but my mother has wound thread around it so that it fits me. 'You must always wear it when you go to court,' she whispered. 'The Empress will be pleased.'

The rozas began just the day after my birthday. And I felt the contrast to Kabul immensely. Not just the heat, but the whole atmosphere is different—the people, the speech, costume, food. Naturally we are more at home here in Agra.

Eid, too, was more like I remembered it as a child.

3 July

Today the Emperor is marrying the daughter of Qazi Isa so there is a festive atmosphere in the whole city. Many important people offer their

daughters in marriage to the Emperor, I have heard. And when suitable, he accepts graciously.

The prospect of another wife hardly ruffles the Padshah Begum. She and Salima Sultana Begum are secure in their positions of favour—a new queen is just another woman in the harem.

I try to imagine what it must feel like, to be the queen of the zenana, to have the power to influence the Emperor himself. Sometimes I feel dispirited, thinking my ambitions are beyond my reach. We have been here for several months, and I have yet to set eyes on the Shehzada.

Two months later

I missed the activity of the court in Kabul. But it's odd how, now that we're back, life seems to have acquired the same monotony of routine. One can tire of the constant chatter of court life too, even with its variety of activities and incidents. Despite the fullness of my days, I am bored and for this reason I have been neglecting to write my diary. It seems there's nothing worth recording.

But the Dussehra celebrations are more than memorable. Our Padshah celebrated the festival with much fanfare along with the gracious Mariam-us-Zamani, his Rajput Begum—Salim's mother. The elephants in the imperial stables— and there is an enormous number of them— were decorated and led out for the Emperor to review. What a magnificent sight it was! The noble beasts with colourful patterns drawn on their heads, brocaded howdahs on their backs, saluting their master by raising their trunks respectfully, offering him garlands of fragrant flowers. The Emperor flung down golden coins for the mahouts and the watching public. Later there was a brilliant display of fireworks similar to the Shab-e-Baraat celebrations.

The festival of Diwali will be celebrated with no less fanfare. The Emperor worships fire as a symbol of light and this Jashn-e-chiragh has a particular appeal for him.

But...I'm beginning to feel it's pointless continuing with this roznamcha...

The Thirty-Eighth Year of the Reign of His Majesty Padshah Abul Fath Jalal-Ud-Din Muhammad Akbar

Lahore, 1594

IT'S BEEN SEVERAL DAYS SINCE I have been walking around like a living corpse. The monsoon sky has come crashing down on my head and I'm struggling to fight my way out of the rubble.

> 'My grief is so great that it has settled in my
> heart like a mountain of ice
> Will the clouds ever part and let the sun's
> rays through to melt it, O Makhfi?*

---

* Pseudonym used by Mughal women

Today, even a poem brings no relief, no balm
for my pain
Only the bitter brine of tears stings my
lacerated heart.'

To whom am I to confide my sorrow but you, my dear roznamcha? I have unearthed you from the depths of my chest but truly, I feel as if I am the one who has been buried alive. To imagine that it was the Padshah Begum, the person I have revered so much, served with such devotion, indeed loved, who brought my world crashing down on my head?

Ammi is not happy either. But who can go against the Emperor's wishes? Worse, I have to continue in my duties to the Empress and pretend all is well. Like a puppet, I nod and try to answer in a normal tone. She is too shrewd not to be aware of my unhappiness.

'What's the matter, Mehr-un-Nissa?' she said sharply yesterday. 'A young girl like you should be jumping around with joy. As it is you are getting quite over age for marriage.'

I tried to smile. 'I am very happy, your

majesty, and very grateful that-that you chose a husband for me.' Hurriedly, I added that. Baba may not have mentioned it, but who else but the Empress could have recommended me as a bride for Ali Quli Khan Istajlu? The very name is bitter in my mouth. 'It is just that it was so sudden. I-I was quite content serving you.'

The Empress laughed, her attendants chimed in dutifully. Sometimes I think we're like echoes, mimicking the Padshah Begum's words. We cannot use our own voices.

She pinched my cheek, so hard that it hurt. 'My pretty one, you will have plenty of opportunity when your husband is away fighting the Emperor's battles.'

A common soldier...if Prince Salim was not meant for me, at least she could have found a courtier, an educated man who could appreciate poetry and music. What value will my education hold for this man, whose only recommendation is that he had distinguished himself in battle?

It is the Khan-i-khana, Abdur Rahim, who holds this man in high esteem. Ali Quli, who

had fled from Persia like us, is said to have fought so well that he contributed to the conquest of Thatta in Sind. Thus, he won the Khan-i-khana's favour, who presented him to the Emperor. The brave soldier was rewarded with a mansabdari of three hundred soldiers.

And a bride. Me.

'He is Persian. Like us,' Baba had said, trying hard to make him sound desirable. Ammi's mouth was set in a thin line. She, too, knew that he was not the right person for me.

But what choice did we have against the Emperor's wish?

A week later

If my engagement was an ordeal, what would my wedding be like?

Mah Banu Banu, Abdur Rahim's wife, took on the role of Ali Quli's mother for the performance of the ceremony. He has no relatives here. She arrived in great style...after all, Abdur Rahim Khan-i-khana is considered the Emperor's stepson because Empress Salima Sultan Begum was his father Bairam Khan's second wife. More so, the great poet is one of the Emperor's navratnas or nine jewels.

Marriage is not supposed to be a meeting of souls, I'm slowly realizing, but a convenient alliance. A girl's wishes do not carry any weight. The Khan-i-khana wants Ali Quli's loyalty. The brave soldier will be very useful in future campaigns, no doubt.

Several platters of gifts followed the Begum—expensive garments and jewels for me, sweets, fruits and dried fruits. I sat there like a stone, as my hand was pledged to this stranger. Luckily, my gold-embroidered veil concealed my expressions effectively.

But despite my repugnance, I forced myself to take a good look at my affianced groom. The rough tones of his voice grated on my ears as he raised his voice in greeting when he entered our courtyard. He loomed over the other men but it did not add to his allure for me. His weather-beaten face, with its furrowed brow, made him look even older than I thought he might be. I remembered Kauser...she too had had to marry against her wishes...but she had found

contentment after the birth of her son. Will my yearning soul find peace in motherhood?

A few days later

This is the month that the Hindus celebrate as Sawan, monsoon. Swings have been put up in the royal gardens and in the evening, the courtyards resound with the strains of the malhar sung by Mian Tansen and his disciples. Usually I am gone by then. But during the day, the Empress calls the singing girls to croon folksongs of the season. Most of them are about being separated from loved ones and their melancholy notes drag me down further.

As I said, the Emperor loves to celebrate all the festivals. He also provides many kinds of diversions for the ladies of the zenana. That's why he has the Meena Bazaar organized every month for three days, an exclusive event where women traders sell goods of all kinds— from fabrics to jewels, fancy rugs to pet birds. The Khushroz, it is called, and the palace ladies shop to their heart's content. It will be held tomorrow. I wish I could make some

excuse to avoid it, but Ruqayya Begum will be displeased.

The next evening

Why is my fate playing tricks with me? O roznamcha, what I am about to tell you should be inscribed in code. I dread that my inquisitive sister Khadija might unearth you from my chest and discover my secret.

As I mentioned, I had no interest left in the Meena Bazaar. What pleasure could pretty clothes and baubles hold for me now? I managed to slip away and sit in a corner of the palace garden, away from the giggling, chattering crowd.

Lost in thoughts of my miserable future, I didn't even notice the imposing figure till he was right in front of me. And when I did, I almost fell off my seat! Prince Salim! Yes, it was him, though it took me a moment to realize it.

It was the jewels adorning the insteps of his brocade shoes that I noticed first. Even the wealthiest of nobles would not flaunt such extravagant rubies and diamonds studded in their footwear. My eyes travelled up to catch sight of the silk qaba with its gold embroidery, embedded with pearls and sapphires, emeralds and topaz. The diamonds and rubies on his fingers dazzled my eyes. After that what else could happen? I was transfixed by the face my eyes had been searching for, for years. That dreamy, heavy-lidded gaze, the sharply etched features, the glossy black moustache accentuating the paleness of his skin. The enormous emerald on his turban...it had to be Prince Salim.

He had a pair of pigeons tucked in the crook of his arm. Even as I was goggling at him from behind my transparent veil, he said in his imperious tone, 'You, girl, hold these for me, while I pluck some roses.'

'Yes, yes, your imperial highness,' I stammered. The tips of my fingers brushed his as he passed the birds to me. I almost fainted on the spot.

'Take care not to let them fly away,' he said. 'They are a special breed.'

I could only nod. My heart was whirling faster than the feet of the most accomplished dancer in court. Salim...at long last. Was this all a dream? Or was my engagement a bad dream? But Salim had not even seen my face, he didn't know who I was. Would he just take back his pigeons and walk away? How could I let that happen!

I nuzzled the silken feathers of the birds. They had been nestling close to his heart and now I held them near mine. Their rapid heartbeat almost outpaced mine. Overwhelmed by the situation, I could barely draw breath. One of the birds squirmed in my grasp and before I knew it, it had slipped out and winged away. I watched it open mouthed as it flew higher and higher and disappeared.

'Girl! What have you done with my pigeon?' That commanding voice again, outraged and furious now. 'You let it get away!'

I should have collapsed on the spot. Don't know what impulse led me to say, with all the innocence I could infuse on my face: 'Like this!' I opened my arms and let the other pigeon escape.

'You...how did you dare? Who are you, you

impertinent creature?' His face was flushed with rage as he flung open my veil.

'My-my name is Mehr-un-nissa,' I said in a small voice. 'Can you forgive me, your highness?' I looked up into his eyes.

Our gazes remained locked for a long time. Finally, he let out a deep breath and said, grasping my hand, 'If you had not been so lovely...I would have had you thrown into the dungeons. Lovely and daring. Mehr-un-nissa... truly a "Sun amongst women". Whose daughter are you, Mehr-un-nissa?'

'Mirza Ghiyas Beg,' I was murmuring when someone cleared their throat loudly. 'Your highness, his majesty your father is calling you.' It was the head eunuch.

'Can't you see I'm busy?'

'Please, your highness...' the eunuch pleaded.

Salim sighed. 'Wait here for me, Mehr-un-nissa,' he whispered.

Before he could return, however, the Empress arrived with her entourage and carried me off.

But he has seen me, and will not forget me

easily. Maybe I can escape this hateful alliance. If Allah wills...

The next evening

Last night I couldn't sleep a wink thinking about him. The way he had gazed at me...as if he was bewitched...he actually held my hand!

If only the eunuch hadn't come, if only Ruqayya Begum hadn't passed that way...but... there's no denying that I've made an impression on him.

My heart was all aflutter as I made my way into the Empress's apartments. Till now, I would be greeted with remarks like, 'So...who visited you in your dreams last night?' 'What kind of dress are you wearing for the nikah?'

I had to summon up a laugh and parry them with words like, 'Wouldn't you like to know?' 'You'll find out!'

Today, however, the usual chatter ceased the moment I entered and made my salaam to the Empress. The awkward silence chilled me, but I said with my usual polite smile, 'I trust all is well with your majesty.'

The Padshah Begum did not smile back. Her tone had more than a touch of asperity as she replied, 'All is well with *me*. I don't know about other people.'

The ladies around her smiled and exchanged meaningful glances. I bit my lip hard. For once I was at a loss for words. If Khurram hadn't climbed onto the Padshah Begum's lap at that moment, who knows which path the exchange would have taken.

I took out the jama I was embroidering for the Empress and made myself unnoticeable in a corner.

A kind of defiance began to build up inside me. 'Wait and see,' I wanted to tell the ladies who flung such disapproving glances at me. 'When Salim says he wants to marry me, you will regret your behaviour.'

But the Empress was not one to spare anybody. I might have been her favourite, but that was not any reason to be easy on me.

'So...what were you doing, sneaking around on your own yesterday? I hear Salim is very annoyed with you for letting his precious

pigeons fly away. They were a very rare breed. If Salima Sultana Begum hadn't intervened, he would have banished you from the fort.' Her attendants tittered.

I kept my gaze down as I replied in a low tone. 'It-it was a mistake, your majesty. The bird wriggled out of my grasp. How could I dare to lose something so precious to the Shehzada?'

'Hmmm...this is not the way I heard it. Watch your step, my girl. The court is a slippery place.' My breath caught in my throat. As I clenched my fist, the sewing needle pierced my finger. I swallowed the cry that rose to my throat. The Empress's words sounded faint and distant. 'You are as good as married. Don't forget that we maintain strict decorum here.'

I pulled myself together to reply, 'Your majesty, please accept my most humble apologies. It was not my intention to flout decorum.'

'Hmmm...go and bring me my paandan. Some silly fool forgot to place it here. And call Sakina to massage my feet!'

I jumped to my feet and ran to fetch the jewel-studded paandan.

A week later

A whole week has gone by and still no news from Salim. A whole week that I haven't been able to sleep.

I cannot marry that lout Ali Quli Istajlu! Surely, I was meant for better things than to live as a common soldier's wife? Desperate thoughts enter my mind. To bribe one of the eunuchs and send a note to Salim. But the problem is you cannot trust anyone. If I put a single step wrong, it could create trouble for my whole family. My father might lose the Emperor's favour. Haven't we all seen what a miserable fate awaits those who are foolish enough to defy the Padshah?

At the palace, I go through my duties mechanically. An insane hope keeps me on edge. Salim knows I wait upon the Empress. He is bound to come here and seek me. But they say...most of the time he lives in a wine- and opium-induced stupor. I don't want to believe it. For me he is the most perfect man in the world.

Some days later

The merchants continue to throng our house,
laden with bales of silk, velvet and brocade.
Their attendants open up the rolls of multi-
hued fabric and unfurl them with a flourish.
Through my veil, I watch dispiritedly and stroke
the fine muslin from Dhaka, the gleaming
Benares brocade as Ammi suggests.

'This scarlet brocade will be perfect for your
wedding ghaghra,' she murmurs.

'What am I going to wear?' Khadija leans
against my shoulder. She is old enough to don
a veil now, but her behaviour remains that of a
seven-year-old.

'This rose pink would be perfect for the
younger sister,' the merchant smiles. His teeth
are deeply stained with paan and his sunken
eyes outlined with surma. 'My fabrics are
sourced from the master weavers. Look how
delicate the zari work is. It will not lose its shine
in a hundred years.'

I want to hurl all the bales of cloth out of
the door. But I smile and murmur vague words
of praise. If only I was marrying Salim, I would

have been walking on air. 'You choose, Ammi,' I say. 'I have a headache.'

Ammi gives me a sharp look. 'Go and lie down. Khadija, ask Dilbagh to rub some balm on your sister's forehead.'

There is no balm that will cure my headache. And my escape lasts just half an hour because a jeweller arrives with velvet-covered boxes for our perusal. Necklaces of gold, sparkling with precious stones, waistbelts, bracelets, bindulis for the forehead and elaborate naths. My head spins just looking at them. 'Just look at this chandrahaar,' the jeweller holds up a dazzling necklace. 'How fine the kundan is! And these jadau karnaphools...how about this satlada—the emeralds in the pendants are the finest you can buy.'

'You choose, Ammi,' I say listlessly, longing to fling off the glittering seven stringed necklace she holds around my neck.

She sighs. 'I'm taking the jadau satlada on approval,' Ammi says to the jeweller. 'And that kundan waistchain.'

I feel that the weight of all that finery has descended on me. Will Allah grant me reprieve?

Two weeks later

The rains have receded and already people are looking forward to the mild weather ahead of us. Rain or sunshine, heat or cold—it makes little difference to me. The landscape of my life is a barren desert right now.

Worse, today I heard something that extinguished the tiny flame of hope that still flickered in my heart.

When the Empress was stretched on her couch, savouring her afternoon nap, one of the slave girls, Gauhar, beckoned to me into a quiet nook.

'Sit, Mehr bibi,' she said gently. 'You are looking very pale these days. I notice that you just peck at your food.'

Her kindness made my eyes fill up. 'The Shehzada is besotted with you,' she whispered. 'He went and asked his father for permission to marry you. But Zille Illahi refused outright, saying that you were already betrothed. The prince ranted and raved, but his father was adamant. He himself had arranged the match, he said, he could not go back on his word.'

My head swam. She pressed my hand sympathetically. I would have fainted then and there if she hadn't furtively splashed water on my face from a surahi placed close by. 'Be careful,' she said. 'Sit up. Sakina has been throwing suspicious glances at us. She would love to know what we're talking about.'

I took a long drink of water. Somehow, I had to pull myself together. I could not let this news destroy me. Surely, Allah had saved me for some important destiny. This had to be a passing test. Gauhar ran and brought me a tall silver glass of rose sherbet. I sipped it slowly.

Finally, I asked, 'Does everyone know?'

She dropped her gaze. 'I'm afraid they do. Such news does not stay hidden long.'

It struck me that my father, probably my brothers, had heard too. What about my mother?

I wished some kind djinn would carry me away, far from Lahore. If I had been a man, I could have taken service as a soldier, ridden off to some distant part of the empire. But being a girl, I am condemned to remain trapped in my cage of sorrow.

Ten days later

The day that I'm dreading fast approaches. There is already a festive atmosphere in our house. Guests are arriving. Saliha is here from distant Kabul, her children race over the whole house playing with little Arjumand.

The singing girls sit with dholaks in our inner courtyard every evening, and the air is filled with the monotonous strains of their wedding songs. Khadija and Manija are encouraged to twirl to their tunes, other friends join in.

Garlands of marigolds, interspersed with glossy green leaves are festooned all over the house. The cooks sit in the backyard, simmering qormas, grilling kebabs, steaming biryanis. Stacks of naans, sheermal and kulchas emerge from the tandoor. Clay saucers of fragrant phirni, steaming halwa, delectable faluda are passed around. The gourmet guests taste the various delicacies and pronounce their opinion.

I am the only one who has no appetite. The days stumble past me. In the frenzy of preparation, it seems, almost everyone has forgotten me. That's the way I want it.

But how can the bride remain forgotten?

Abul, who has always been closest to me among my siblings, finds an opportunity to draw me aside from the crowd one day. 'Mehru,' he says, his eyes soft with sympathy, 'try and accept what is inevitable.' Then he sighed deeply. 'I have heard that the Shehzada pleaded with the Emperor. But he had already given his word. Ali Quli is not a bad man. He will go far in life. Please... my sweet sister.' He squeezed my hand gently.

I could only nod. Heaven knows I'm far from sweet...

A few days later

I don't know when I'll manage to snatch a few moments to share my feelings with you next, my roznamcha. The first few streaks of light are brightening the room. I have lain awake all night. Perhaps it'll relieve my heartache somewhat to put my ordeal down on paper.

Today was the manjha ceremony. Ammi had dressed me in a yellow satin gharara for the event. They said it brightened up my pale face.

This is what I have to hear all the time. That I am just skin and bone now. That I need to eat nourishing food.

But my appetite has totally deserted me...

I sat like a puppet as my sisters and friends rubbed turmeric paste on my arms and legs. The singing girls kept tune to their lively songs on hand drums and dholaks. Laughter and revelry filled the air around me. But despite Abul's sensible advice, I just couldn't reconcile myself to what was happening. This has to be a bad dream, I kept telling myself.

Since my parents had to flee their native land, we have few close relatives here. But both Baba and Ammi have a host of friends, won by their warmth and hospitality. I cannot hope to carry this affectionate atmosphere to my marital home. My future husband is an uncouth person, a rough and ready soldier. He is adept with his sword, but elegant phrases will never cross his lips.

The worst is, recently I discovered that he used to be a safarchi or table attendant to the Persian king. And to think my ancestors were

aristocrats, my grandfather a highly acclaimed poet. This man is considered a good match for me. How arbitrary are the whims of emperors! We are but pawns in their games.

I should scratch this out. It could be the death of me if someone discovered my diary. Someone who wished my family ill. I don't know how many such people there are in this city. But why take a chance...

A week later

Reconnecting with my roznamcha in my marital home is like finding an old friend. And I badly need one. Luckily, I had the good sense to hide it inside a cushion and to insist that I would not be able to sleep without this particular pillow. But till now I have not dared to unearth it. Actually, there hasn't been much time either.

Barely five days have passed since my rukhsati took place. My whole family wept as my brothers helped me into the palanquin. Behind my red gold-embroidered veil, I watched Baba helplessly brushing away his constantly flowing tears. Ammi and my sisters sobbed helplessly.

I was the only one dry eyed. No doubt it must have caused much talk. But I have placed a huge rock over my heart. That's the only way I can survive.

Memories of my nikah flash across my mind as I lean back on the bolster and huddle in my pashmina shawl. Chill winds have already begun to sweep through the city. The qazi asking for my consent...my voice was fainter than usual. My husband's voice rang through the room, making me start. I had no interest in looking at his face in my arsi—the small mirror in my thumb ring. I had already seen him at the engagement and in any case, the golden strands of his sehra were an effective veil.

Mah Banu Begum welcomed me into my marital home, holding the holy Quran over my head as a blessing. There are congratulatory voices all around. For once I'm grateful for the veil that hides my expression.

The next two days of my wedded life are a total blank in my mind. Dilbagh had accompanied me, according to custom. She helped me set up my new home. We had the Persian carpets

my parents gifted me unrolled, paintings were hung on the walls, embroidered bolsters placed on the silver-lined takhts. However, no matter how hard we tried, the place could not match the warmth of home.

And just this morning my husband left on a campaign in Rajasthan with Prince Salim of all people. I didn't know whether to be happy or sad.

It was after Dilbagh left, trying to suppress her sobs, that a kind of acceptance descended on me finally. It was like a truce with my destiny. Maybe I was passing through the stage the Hindu astrologers described as the seven-and-a half years of bad luck.

I cannot help remembering my friend Kauser who had no choice but to be the second wife of an elderly man. Once her son was born, she found new joy in her existence. Maybe...when I have children...it'll be different.

One of the maids is standing here, watching me...I repeat a couplet as if I am in the midst of composing one. Then smile and ask her to fetch a glass of ginger tea.

A week later

I'm getting the uneasy feeling that this slave girl Rukhsana has been placed here by my husband to spy on me while he's away.

The first inkling I got was when he asked me one evening after he had returned from the court, three days after our wedding, 'So, how have been whiling away the time, Begum? Composing poetry? I hear you have already acquired quite a reputation at this young age.'

There was something mocking about his laugh. It went through me like a knife.

'Sahib, I'm not sure about having a reputation for poetry,' I replied calmly as I served some mutton shorba into a bowl for him. 'But you know I belong to a family of poets. It certainly helps to pass the time pleasantly.'

'Hmm...well, the Empress has asked if I can spare you occasionally to attend on her.' His eyes pierced me. 'We cannot refuse her majesty's commands but I trust you know how to conduct yourself decently, now that you're a married woman.'

My face grew hot. I would have given him

a stinging response but I was conscious of the slave girl standing there with a smirk on her face. 'I will surely attend to her majesty,' I said indifferently. 'She is the epitome of decorum as every regular in court knows. Rukhsana, bring some more sheermal!' I said sharply. 'This girl is very slow in performing her duties.'

His face darkened. I squashed down the wave of sadness that was swelling in my chest, recalling the laughter around our dastarkhwan at home...

The Thirty-Ninth Year of the Reign of His Majesty Padshah Abul Fath Jalal-Ud-Din Muhammad Akbar

Lahore, January 1595

WHAT A LONG GAP IT HAS BEEN, my roznamcha! You can imagine to what depths of misery I had sunk if I could not even summon up the enthusiasm to note down the mundane details of my routine. I have been storing it all in my head. After that incident when he mocked me for writing poetry, despite all my efforts to rally my spirits, I could hardly bear to put pen to paper.

I was shocked to find myself turning petty, picking on the servants, especially on Rukhsana. Sometimes I made her massage my feet all through the afternoon till she drooped with fatigue. Once I pushed her slyly when she was serving a cup of wine to my husband so it spilled on his silk qaba. He sprang up with rage and slapped her. I'm ashamed to share that I exulted inwardly.

When the Empress sent a palanquin for me one day, I started up with joy. I dressed with great care in one of my trousseau outfits. Lined my eyes thickly with kaajal and chewed some paan to redden my lips. Salim would not be there to admire me but the ladies of Ruqayya's entourage should be aware that my looks had not faded with marriage.

'Ah...there she comes...my Eid ki Chand!' The Empress squashed me in her embrace.

'If your majesty had commanded me...I would have run here the day after my nikah,' I smiled.

'As quick witted as ever!' the Padshah Begum

cackled. 'How I have missed you…but I am not inconsiderate as to part a pair of turtle doves.'

'Your majesty is always so kind,' I murmured.

'How pretty she looks,' one of the ladies cooed as she leaned forward to embrace me. She inhaled deeply. 'What is this heavenly fragrance? Is it one of your mother's concoctions?'

My smile was spontaneous. 'Indeed, it is. She created some new attars for my wedding.'

'How talented she is! But I would like to add—like mother like daughter,' the lady arched an eyebrow.

I bent low and salaamed my thanks. What a relief it was to be out of that dismal house. But I little knew that further misery was in store for me.

I can hear footsteps coming close to my door. I should hide my diary…

It was only the new slave girl. She is meek and compliant, unlike Rukhsana, who I was able to get rid of. How wickedly manipulative I've become! During those happy, innocent days in my father's house, could I ever have imagined that I could think of using my own misfortune to destroy another human being?

But how bitter I was...when that one hope for happiness I had been clutching at, was snatched away from me.

It was just a few days after I began going to the palace again that I had a spell of dizziness. Bouts of nausea followed. The slave girls exchanged knowing glances, but I dared not believe what my heart proclaimed. When Ammi came to visit me one day, I hesitantly shared my symptoms.

'Allah be praised!' she raised her hands to the sky gratefully. 'Be very careful now, child. I will ask the Padshah Begum to excuse you from your duties at the palace. Have you told your husband?'

'I-I didn't want to say anything till I was sure.' I stammered.

'Don't waste any time now. Tell him this very evening.'

I whispered the news to him that night, hoping that my hesitation would be interpreted as bashfulness. His joy was frightening. 'Ah Begum! The one above has blessed our union.' His eyes had an alarming glitter as he gazed at me. 'I want a troop of children running around this house. And we will! Won't we?' He embraced me with a gentleness he had never displayed earlier.

That night I felt there was some hope for us after all. Little did I know what a fool's paradise I was living in.

Because...barely a couple of months later, it happened. A miserable rainy day...a month ago. Ammi had come with Khadija and Manija to see how I was feeling, laden with sweets as usual.

After they left, feeling a little tired, I decided to lie down. I don't know how my foot slipped. Or did I trip on something? A fold in the carpet? And when I fell, an unbearable pain cramped up from my thighs to my belly. I must have cried aloud because that woman Rukhsana appeared right away. She was followed by another slave girl. The two of them helped me up, but by then, the blood had begun to seep out, staining my dress, the carpet and my heart.

Was it the extremity of my sorrow that led me to blame Rukhsana for the wrinkled carpet? I can't write any more...

A week later

The moment I had recovered somewhat, Sher Afgan donned his armour, picked up his weapons and set off on another campaign. His eyes glittered with excitement at the prospect of fresh opportunities to demonstrate his valour and earn more laurels.

God bless him, he is an ambitious man, my husband.

I bade goodbye to him with prayers for his safety and said I would miss him. But in my heart of hearts, I was glad to see him go. The moment he mounted his horse, bearing his loud voice, his anger and his restless energy away, a welcome peace descended on the house. What a blessing to be left to my own devices! However, a spasm of bitterness did shoot through my heart, recalling how my own parents could never bear to be separated.

And...Sher Afgan had shown little sympathy for my suffering at the loss of our baby, rather he had ranted against what he described as my 'carelessness'.

But I should explain his new title. Ali Quli

acquired it during the Rajasthan campaign, though not in actual battle: Sher Afgan or 'tiger slayer'.

Any other wife would have been bursting with pride at the reputation that he has acquired, the promotion in status and the rich rewards in gold. But more than pride, it is gratitude I feel.

Because...he saved Salim's life.

During the journey, they happened to glimpse some tiger cubs in a forest. The prince, fascinated with animals as he is, dismounted to pick them up. Within minutes the mother appeared and hurled herself on him. The ferocity of the animal, the suddenness of the attack stunned his guards, who were unable to act immediately. It was my fearless husband who leapt onto the fierce animal and slashed her to death with his sword.

Thus, he saved the life of the Wali Ahad—the crown prince. You can imagine how overwhelmed with gratitude Salim was, and how effusively the rest of the party lauded my husband. Immediately, the Shehzada

proclaimed that henceforth he would be known as 'Sher Afgan'.

As for me, though I cannot call myself faint-hearted, I almost collapsed onto the ground when I heard about this hair-raising incident. There is no denying that my husband displayed courage miles above the ordinary. Everyone says he will reach great heights on the strength of his feats.

If only I could love him!

But dear roznamcha, I've come to the conclusion that there's no point shedding futile tears. If, as a helpless babe, I could survive the coils of a fearful snake, surely as an adult, I can battle the vagaries of fortune? Someday, my saviour will come, my angel with a flaming sword, to rescue me. Till then, there is the love of my family, laughter, painting and poetry and so much more to enjoy!

> *'The hot wind blows dust into my eyes,*
> *My tears wash it out and my vision clears*
> *I can see gardens blooming for my delight*
> *Scent the fragrant flowers strewn on my path.'*

The Real Nur Jahan in History

NUR JAHAN WAS THE TWENTIETH WIFE of Emperor
Jahangir and the most powerful empress in
Mughal history. She is considered to have
been the de facto ruler during Jahangir's reign,
managing the affairs of state with consummate
skill. The fact that she had coins minted in her
name, and accompanied the emperor on his
'jharoka darshan' or 'balcony viewing', is proof
enough of her status and the extent of her
influence over Jahangir.

Nur Jahan was not only efficient in
administration but also a woman with a highly
developed aesthetic sense. She was a talented
poet and deeply interested in music and art.

Architecture was another of her passions and the impressive monuments she designed and constructed along with beautiful gardens, pay tribute to the impressive range of her abilities.

The story of her life is extraordinary too. Nur Jahan was born in Kandahar on 31 May 1577 and named Mehr-un-nissa by her parents. Her father Mirza Ghiyas Beg and his wife Asmat Begum both hailed from aristocratic Persian families. Ghiyas Beg's father Muhammad Sharif held important positions under Shah Tahmasp Safawi and he and his older brother Muhammad Tahir were highly reputed poets. But Ghiyas Beg was compelled to flee the land of his birth when his father died and he fell out of favour with the current ruler.

Mirza Ghiyas Beg headed towards India with his pregnant wife and three children, to seek his fortune in Emperor Akbar's court. The dramatic incident of Mehr-un-Nissa's birth has already been narrated in the story. Ghiyas Beg's benefactor, Malik Masud, presented him to the emperor, who was impressed by the Persian's refined bearing and awarded him a mansab of

300 soldiers. Ghiyas Beg rose fast in Akbar's favour and was appointed the diwan or treasurer in Kabul—an important position.

Apart from the dramatic story of her birth and rescue, not too much is known about Nur Jahan's childhood and adolescence, so this diary is entirely fictional, except for real historical events. However, she must have led a comfortable life in Agra and Fatehpur Sikri where her father owned houses and later in Lahore where Akbar shifted his court in 1585. Historical accounts mention two older brothers, Muhammad Sharif and Abul Hasan, later known as Asaf Khan, and two younger sisters Khadija and Manija and a younger brother Shahpur. Like other girls from aristocratic families, Mehr-un-nissa was well educated at home by tutors in subjects like history, literature, mathematics, art and music. She also became proficient in her mother tongue Persian as well as Turki—the language of the Mughals— and Arabic. Her grandfather and uncle had been highly regarded poets; Nur Jahan was to display considerable talent in that field as well.

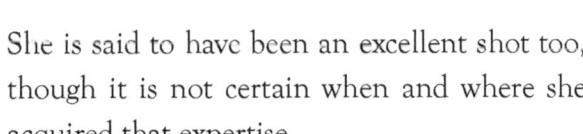

She is said to have been an excellent shot too, though it is not certain when and where she acquired that expertise.

The romance between Nur Jahan and Jahangir is almost as famous in Mughal history as the one between Shah Jahan and Mumtaz Mahal, who was Nur Jahan's niece—the daughter of her brother Abul Hasan. It is not certain when Mehr-un-nissa met the future emperor and cast her spell on him. There are conflicting accounts of their first encounter, mostly in the writings of foreign travellers. The story of the pigeons that I have mentioned is the most famous one, though there is another about Prince Salim coming upon her in the palace garden and yet another about catching a glimpse of her in a boat on the river Ravi in Lahore.

Whatever the truth, Mehr-un-nissa had to undergo some difficult times before she reached the exalted status of Empress Nur Jahan. In 1594, when she was seventeen, Emperor Akbar arranged her marriage with Ali Quli Istajlu, a Persian mercenary. Ali Quli had acquired a reputation for his courage in battle

and martial skills, though he had originally been a table attendant to Shah Ismail II of Persia and fled the country when the ruler was assassinated. Abdur Rahim Khan-i-Khana, the Emperor's stepbrother and one of his nine gems, recommended Ali Quli to the emperor after witnessing his daring feats in battle. Akbar granted a mansab to the soldier and found a bride for him as well. After his marriage to Mehr-un-nissa, Ali Quli accompanied Prince Salim in his campaign against the Rana of Udaipur. Jahangir has mentioned in his memoirs that he awarded the title Sher Afgan or 'tiger slayer' to the Persian soldier for his bravery. Accounts vary as to the exact date this happened, though historian Ellison Banks Findly has mentioned the date as 1599. Thus, at that time, Mehr-un-nissa's husband was in favour with Prince Salim. Later, however, when Salim rebelled against his father Akbar, Sher Afgan kept faith with the emperor and subsequently, it is said, he joined the conspiracy to put Salim's son Khusrau on the throne, along with Raja Man Singh and Mirza Aziz Koka.

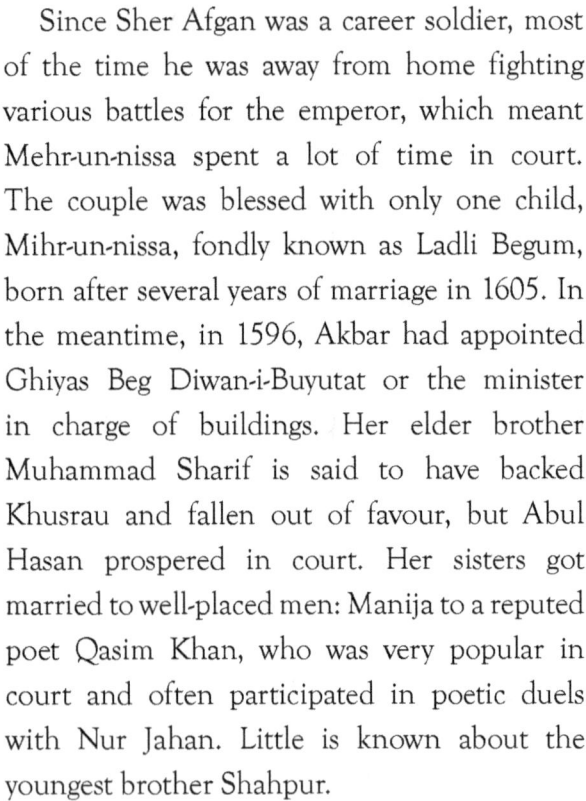

Since Sher Afgan was a career soldier, most of the time he was away from home fighting various battles for the emperor, which meant Mehr-un-nissa spent a lot of time in court. The couple was blessed with only one child, Mihr-un-nissa, fondly known as Ladli Begum, born after several years of marriage in 1605. In the meantime, in 1596, Akbar had appointed Ghiyas Beg Diwan-i-Buyutat or the minister in charge of buildings. Her elder brother Muhammad Sharif is said to have backed Khusrau and fallen out of favour, but Abul Hasan prospered in court. Her sisters got married to well-placed men: Manija to a reputed poet Qasim Khan, who was very popular in court and often participated in poetic duels with Nur Jahan. Little is known about the youngest brother Shahpur.

When Salim finally ascended the throne as Jahangir in 1605, he raised Ghiyas Beg to the position of Diwan of the empire along with Wazir Khan. He also granted him the title Itmad-ud-daula or 'pillar of state'. Generously, Jahangir pardoned many of the men who had

conspired against him, including Sher Afgan. He appointed him to an important post—subedar or governor of Bardhwan in Bengal. But Sher Afgan was still embroiled in the conspiracy to place Khusrau on the throne. However, once again, the prince was defeated. His sympathizers were exposed and in 1607, the emperor sent his foster brother Qutab-ud-din Koka to Bengal as governor and asked him to summon Sher Afgan to court. When Koka came to meet Sher Afgan, he attacked and killed him and was slain in turn.

Widowed now, and in a difficult position as the wife of a conspirator, Mehr-un-nissa and her daughter returned to Jahangir's court where she lived under the protection of Ruqayya Begum, Akbar's wife, who was extremely fond of her. After four years, in 1611, Jahangir is said to have encountered Mehr-un-nissa at the Meena Bazaar set up as part of the lavish Nauroze or New Year celebrations at court. Meena Bazaars were regularly organized at the Mughal court as entertainment for the harem ladies. On such occasions they remained unveiled and

the emperor would be the only man present. Apparently, when he set eyes on her, the old flame was rekindled. Jahangir decided she would be his twentieth and last wife, and within two months they were married. She was renamed Nur Mahal or 'Light of the Palace'. When she began to demonstrate her many qualities, five years later she received the title Nur Jahan or 'Light of the World'. She also received many jagirs as gifts and would become as fabulously wealthy as the other Mughal empresses before her.

Nur Jahan was obviously not the typical begum of the Mughal harem or zenana, content to spend her time in what were considered womanly pursuits. She had a keen, intelligent mind and she was too well aware of the intrigues rampant in the Mughal court. The Mughal empire was at the height of its power and prosperity at that time, as is obvious from the accounts of travellers from the West, who were dazzled by the wealth and the opulent lifestyle the ruling classes displayed. Jahangir, though a well-intentioned monarch, was addicted

to wine and opium, which had already led his brothers to an early end. Having assessed the situation, within a short time, Nur Jahan took a firm grasp of the affairs of state. She became the emperor's chief adviser and policy maker, outwitting all the factions maneuvering against her. Soon, she was putting the seal on the orders or farmans of the emperor, deciding on appointments to important positions, receiving foreign emissaries and negotiating with foreign merchants. Jahangir relied on her completely and she in turn worked for the welfare of the people and country. She took great care of the emperor's health as well, which was deteriorating because of his lifestyle. As her power grew, her family prospered, her brother Abul Hasan receiving the title Asaf Khan, while her father continued to enjoy the emperor's favour.

If Nur Jahan's skills in administration were not enough, she was also adept at the art of warfare, extremely courageous and a good shot. She is credited with killing two tigers with one shot each. She was apparently adept at planning military campaigns as well. In 1626, when Mahabat Khan, one of Jahangir's favourite generals turned traitor and captured him, holding him hostage in Kabul, Nur Jahan successfully used both daring and guile to free her husband.

The couple did not have any children together but Nur Jahan is said to have been fond of her stepson Prince Khurram, who ascended the Mughal throne as Shah Jahan. Khurram was married to her niece Arjumand Bano, later known as Mumtaz Mahal, for whom he built the Taj Mahal. To retain power, Nur Jahan had attempted to arrange a match between her daughter Ladli and Khusrau, Jahangir's eldest son, without success. Eventually Ladli wed Shahryar, his youngest. When Jahangir died in 1627, Nur Jahan tried to capture the throne for Shahryar but was unsuccessful. Her enemies backed the more competent Khurram and her brother Abul Hasan, naturally supported his son-in-law. Shahryar was killed along with other Mughal princes as per the orders of Shah Jahan.

Shah Jahan banished Nur Jahan from the Mughal court and after that she and Ladli led a quiet life in Lahore.

Nur Jahan passed away in 1645, but left an extraordinary legacy behind. Not only had she demonstrated that a woman could rule a huge empire efficiently, but also pursue a variety of causes. She had been a patron to women poets, supported women in need throughout her life and one of her favourite projects was arranging for the marriage of orphaned girls.

Nur Jahan was one of those rare beings blessed with a highly developed aesthetic sense, apart from her aptitude for government. She had a great interest in architecture and Jahangir's exquisite mausoleum in Lahore and the tomb of her father Itmad-ud-daulah in Agra, are among the most magnificent examples of her mastery of design. Her father's tomb took six years to complete and Nur Jahan used her own funds in its construction. Itmad-ud-daula's tomb is said to be the first Mughal structure built of marble; they had always used red sandstone earlier. White is said to have been Nur Jahan's favourite

colour and the pietra dura inlay work in semi-precious stones, also a first in the country, was sourced from Persian designs. This tomb became the inspiration for the more famous Taj Mahal.

Nur Jahan and Jahangir also built mosques and enchanting gardens. Jahangir's Shalimar Garden in Kashmir stands witness to their exquisite taste and the Pathar Masjid in Srinagar is Nur Jahan's contribution. The Nur Afshan (Light Scattering) garden in Agra is the first she planned, among the oldest recognizable Mughal gardens in India, completed probably in 1619. She also designed the Nur Manzil (Abode of Light) and Moti Bagh (Garden of Pearls), in Agra, and the Shah Dara (Royal Threshold) in Lahore which surrounds her husband's tomb. These gardens, with their artistically placed flowering shrubs and trees, fountains and waterfalls, provided a private space for relaxation for the imperial couple and their near ones. Here they could be cooled by gentle breezes even in the scorching heat of summer in Agra, as they sat and read, painted or wrote poetry. Equally fascinating are the

inns or serais Nur Jahan constructed, like the spectacular Nur Mahal Serai near Jullundur. Foreign visitors have remarked on the efficient management of these serais, with resting places for approximately 500 horses and 2,000 travellers. All kinds of facilities were available at nominal cost, safety was ensured and she even had gardens planted beside them.

Nur Jahan's love of the arts extended to poetry, painting and embroidery. It is reported that she was quick at repartee and adept at composing verses on the spot. While it was fashionable for Mughal women to write poetry, living in purdah as they did, they did not use their own names but the pseudonym 'Makhfi' meaning 'the hidden one'. One such couplet attributed to Nur Jahan is connected with an incident when Jahangir appeared wearing a garment on which rubies were used in place of buttons. Nur Jahan wittily proclaimed:

> *It is not the ruby you wear on your robe,*
> *It is a drop of my blood that has seized you by*
> *the collar.*

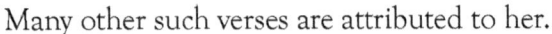

Many other such verses are attributed to her.

The art of miniature painting thrived in Jahangir's court, keeping up an important Mughal tradition and adding to it. Nur Jahan is also credited with inventing many styles of embroidery, still immensely popular today, like badla or mukaish in which silvery strips of metal are used to create delicate patterns and the famous chikankari. Apparently, after her first husband's death, while she was living under Ruqayya Begum's patronage in the court, she supported herself with designing and embroidering outfits for the ladies of the court. Certain styles of pajama, peshwaz or the loose, transparent robes women wore on top of their cholis are said to be designed by her. If it were not enough, she is also credited with many recipes in the Mughlai tradition!

The Mughal harem or zenana has been the source of much curiosity and speculation. It turned into a well-organized institution in the time of Akbar when he constructed the city of Fatehpur Sikri and the nomadic Mughals began to lead more settled lives in palaces rather

than tents. Around five thousand women inhabited Akbar's zenana. They were his wives, concubines and dependent relatives, along with their attendants and slave girls, not to mention the singing and dancing girls who provided entertainment and the eunuchs who supervised the harem. The women had their own rooms and apartments according to their status. The Padshah Begum or the chief wife had the highest status. However, a daughter, Jahanara, enjoyed this position during Shah Jahan's and later her brother Aurangzeb's reign.

Though enclosed behind high walls, there were gardens with ponds and fountains in the complex for the women's relaxation. The area was secured heavily, with mounted soldiers on duty outside and the urdubegis or armed female guards within it. These were usually tall, well-built women from Kashmir, Central Asia or Africa. Eunuchs also performed the same duty. The Nazir-e-mahal or Mahaldar was the person in charge, usually a eunuch, and written reports were submitted regularly to the emperor. There was also a network of spies who kept an eye on the goings on and provided secret reports. No outsider could enter on pain of death. It was the responsibility of the women guards to maintain order within the zenana and resolve the quarrels that often broke out.

Ladies from highly placed families were designated as darogas or supervising officers. It was a position of honour and Asmat Begum, Nur Jahan's mother, once occupied it. The women, while confined, enjoyed many privileges. They received excellent salaries according to their status and the members of the royal family were immensely wealthy. Apart from the revenue from their numerous properties, the leading begums owned ships and traded widely. They spent their money on fancy clothes and jewellery, threw lavish parties, constructed gardens and mosques and also gave generously to charity. The Mughal women were well educated and pursued a variety of interests. For example, at Akbar's request, Babur's daughter Gulbadan Begum wrote *Humayunama*, which records the history of her times but also describes life in the harem from the inside. Many others composed poetry and were interested in painting. Though they were veiled in public, they went on pilgrimage, visited shrines and picnicked in gardens. They also contributed their opinions openly in court from behind the screens that kept them hidden, and helped to resolve quarrels. The zenana was also a hotbed of intrigue where the ladies plotted and manipulated to keep their favourite princes and nobles in power.

Nur Jahan is buried in Lahore in the Shahdara Gardens, close to her husband Jahangir's tomb. Her epitaph reads: 'On the grave of this poor stranger, let there be neither lamp nor rose. Let neither butterfly's wing burn nor nightingale sing.' The fascinating facts of her life continue to keep her memory alive, while her monuments and other contributions stand witness to her numerous talents.

Further Reading

To find out more about Nur Jahan and the Mughal period, here's a list of books I consulted.

Fazl, Abul, *Ain-i-Akbari* or 'Constitution of Akbar', translated by H. Blochman, Baptist Mission Press, 1873, Calcutta

Findly, Ellison Banks, *Nur Jahan: Empress of India*, Oxford University Press New York, 1993

Jafa, Jyoti, *Nurjahan: A Historical Novel*, Writers Workshop, Kolkata, 1978 (later published by Roli Books)

Lal, Ruby, *The Astonishing Reign of Nur Jahan*, Penguin Viking, 2018

Mukhoty, Ira, *Daughters of the Sun, Empresses, Queens and Begums of the Mughal Empire*, Aleph Book Company, New Delhi, 2018

Tuzuk-i-Jahangiri or Memoirs of Jahangir, Gutenberg Press eBook